I0591655

Double Bogeys

Can Kill

Bob Doerr

Jim West mystery/thriller™

TotalRecall Publications, Inc.
1103 Middlecreek
Friendswood, Texas 77546
281-992-3131   281-482-5390 Fax
www.totalrecallpress.com

All rights reserved. Except as permitted under the United States Copyright
Act of 1976, No part of this publication may be reproduced, stored in a
retrieval system, or transmitted in any form or by any means electronic or
mechanical or by photocopying, recording, or otherwise without prior
permission of the publisher. Exclusive worldwide content publication /
distribution by TotalRecall Publications, Inc.

Copyright © 2022 by: Bob Doerr
All rights reserved
ISBN: 978-1-64883-166-9
UPC: 6-43977-41669-8

Library of Congress Control Number: 2022940858

FIRST EDITION
1   2   3   4   5   6   7   8   9   10

This is a work of fiction. The characters, names, events, views, and subject
matter of this book are either the author's imagination or are used
fictitiously. Any similarity or resemblance to any real people, real situations
or actual events is purely coincidental and not intended to portray any
person, place, or event in a false, disparaging or negative light.

The scanning, uploading and distribution of this book via the Internet or via
any other means without the permission of the publisher is illegal and
punishable by law. Please purchase only authorized electronic editions, and
do not participate in or encourage electronic piracy of copyrighted materials.
Your support of the author's rights is appreciated.

TO ALL THE GOLFERS OUT THERE LIKE ME
WHO CAN'T PUTT.

Award Winning Author: Bob Doerr

Award winning author Bob Doerr grew up in a military family, graduated from the Air Force Academy, and had a career of his own in the Air Force. Bob specialized in criminal investigations and counterintelligence gaining significant insight to the worlds of crime, espionage, and terrorism. His work brought him into close coordination with the security agencies of many countries and filled his mind with the fascinating plots and characters found in his books today. His education credits include a Masters in International Relations from Creighton University. A full time author with seventeen published books, Bob was selected by the Military Writers Society of America as its Author of the Year for 2013. The Eric Hoffer Awards awarded *No One Else to Kill* its 2013 first runner up to the grand prize for commercial fiction. Two of his other books were finalists for the Eric Hoffer Award in earlier contests. *Loose Ends Kill* won the 2011 Silver medal for Fiction/mystery by the Military Writers Society of America. *Another Colorado Kill* received the same Silver medal in 2012 and the Silver medal for general fiction at the Branson Stars and Flags national book contest in 2012. In addition to *Double Bogeys Can Kill*, Bob has written eight prior novels in the Jim West series. Bob lives in Garden Ridge, Texas, with Leigh, his wife of 49 years, and Cinco, their ornery cat.

About The Book

Double Bogeys Can Kill is the 9th Jim West mystery/thriller. In this book West finds himself in Myrtle Beach joining 15 retired air force pilots, to fill a void and allow the group to have four foursomes. The week, usually fun and something the pilots look forward to, quickly turns into tragedy as one of the golfers is murdered after the first day of golf. The pilots know West's background as a criminal investigator in the air force and lean on him to solve the murder. The Myrtle Beach police also learn of West's background and want him to be their inside man. West doesn't want the role, knowing it's a lose-lose proposition. He's right, and on the second night, the murderer seeing West as a threat tries to kill him. West survives but requires a trip to the hospital. The suspect pool shrinks down to his fellow golfers. Balancing his cooperation with the police with his golf is not easy as the whole group starts to turn on itself. Finally, West is confronted by the killer now crazy enough to kill himself and take West with him.

Chapter 1

Doug Nelson chipped another yellow Srixon golf ball out of the sand and onto the practice green.

"There you go," he said to himself as the ball rolled close to the flag. "Where was that shot today?"

Twice today, it had taken him two shots to get out of a bunker or what he grew up calling a sand trap. Both times it resulted in his scoring a double bogey, and as every golfer knows, double bogeys can kill your score. His sixteen-handicap didn't give him bragging rights back home, but with this group, it put him near the top, and he liked that position.

He climbed up onto the green, retrieved his balls, and returned to the sand for one last round of practice shots. His first shot went sailing out of the trap and over the green.

"Damn."

A squirrel darted away from the side of the green as an approaching shadow got his attention. Doug turned to look into the setting sun. Despite the glare, he recognized the person.

"You coming out to practice, too?"

He didn't wait for an answer. He knew the answer since he saw the golf club. At least he thought he knew the answer. Doug felt the impact of the first strike as the seven-iron slammed against his right ear. He went down on one knee.

"What the –," his words were cut off with another blow to the top of the head. He didn't fall, remaining there on one knee, and despite the desire, he couldn't move. A third and then a fourth blow came before Doug collapsed onto the sand and died.

Chapter 2

"Chicks dig a milkman," Pete said, grinning ear to ear. The guys around Pete at the table laughed, but I had heard it a dozen times earlier on the course as Pete had explained his wearing of the well-worn, Borden Milk, baseball cap.

Okay, I may have thought it was cute the first time I heard it, too, but it was getting tiresome, and the "chicks" he flirted with on the course were too young to remember milk being delivered door to door. Of course, now all sorts of groceries could be ordered for home delivery, so who knows?

"Let's order," Tom said. "We don't need to wait for Doug."

"Let me call him," Frank said. "He should be on the way." He pressed a few buttons on his phone and put it up to his ear. Frank had been with the group longer than most.

The group of golfers consisted of sixteen retired air force officers, all but me former pilots. They accepted me well enough. My link to the group came through three former F-4, and later F-16, pilots whom I had met early in my own air force career during my tour of duty in Spain. I knew a fourth from my days at the Air Force Academy. Everyone was retired from the military now, although most still worked in other jobs.

They had invited me once before when they could only fill thirteen of their sixteen slots. I surprised myself back then by agreeing to join them. This time they only needed one outsider to fill their quota, so I was impressed they chose me. They were all good guys and just as important, not very good golfers.

"Hey, Doug," Frank said into his phone and then paused. The grin on his face disappeared. "How about you telling me who you are." He looked around at the group, and I could see his eyes widen. "I'm Frank Derby. I'm at the Waffles and Shakes next to the hotel." He paused, listening. "I'll be here. We'll be here."

"What's happening?" Tom asked when Frank put his phone down.

"Doug is dead."

"What?" Mike asked.

"He's dead. That was the police. We're to stay here, and someone will be coming right over to talk to us."

"That means he was murdered," Mike said.

I wanted to say maybe not, but kept quiet as all their eyes now turned and looked at me.

Chapter 3

Their looks weren't accusatory. They all knew that I had dealt with murders before, and they hadn't. I had seen similar looks in the past. While I never understood why people expected me to do anything, at least I had become accustomed to "the look."

"Frank, what did they say? I mean how?" Pete asked.

"They didn't. He said he couldn't come to the phone."

"Then how do you know he's dead?' Pete asked.

"I heard someone else in the background ask how long has he been dead or something like that."

"Jesus, he can't be dead. His daughter is getting married next week," Mike said.

"When did anyone see him last?" Frank asked.

"In the club house after the round," Pete said, and everyone agreed.

Only five of us sat together in the restaurant. Not counting Doug, who should've been with us, the other ten golfers in the group had gone elsewhere for their dinner.

"He didn't come to the meeting either," I said.

"Yeah, that wasn't like him," Frank said. "I mean people sometimes skip the meeting if they had a bad day, but I thought Doug played well today."

"He did. He shot a ninety-three. Not quite ready for the pro circuit, but for us, not bad," Tom said.

"I can't believe he's dead," Pete said.

A server came to our table, and Frank said we had changed

our mind and would be leaving. "Let's wait for them outside," he said to the rest of us. We all agreed.

A few seconds after we stepped out of the restaurant, a Myrtle Beach Police Department sedan pulled up next to us. A male and a female officer stepped out of the vehicle. They both looked like weight lifters. The man had jet black hair cut in a flat-top and close to the sides of his head. His face had a square flat look, and his neck strained against his shirt collar. While I'm no expert, something about how his arms and neck looked didn't seem natural. I couldn't help but wonder if the MBPD had a steroid problem.

The female officer, coming out of the passenger door approached us first. I could see the muscles in her arms, and her shoulders also stretched out her uniform blouse, but nothing about her gave me any feeling that she might mess with supplements or steroids. She had a nice smile, and her blond hair was cut shoulder length.

"One of you guys Frank Derby?" she asked.

"Me," Frank said.

"The rest of you part of the golf group?"

"Yes, ma'am," Pete said. "Is Doug really dead?"

"Let us ask the questions," the male cop said.

"And you are?" I asked.

He looked at me like I ignored his last statement.

"Let's start over again. I'm Officer Louise Strong, and my partner is Officer Whip Miller. We're here simply to get your names and ask you a few basic questions. One of the detectives will follow-up with more questions later. They should have the answers you're looking for. We don't."

"Then please ask away," I said.

"Why don't you take those three, Whip, and I'll handle these two." Louise chose Frank and me as her two.

Louise had to be the senior officer in the duo, I thought. She led us away from the others a few paces but made no effort to separate the two of us from each other.

"Can you give me your names?"

"I'm Jim West," I said, and Frank identified himself.

"Your hotel and room number?" Louise asked. We gave them to her. "Your phone numbers?" We both answered.

"Do either of you know who might have had a reason to hurt Mr. Nelson? Doesn't have to be someone in the group." We didn't. She gave us her card and asked us to call her if we thought of anything before the detectives got to us.

"Officer Strong, is there anything you can tell us?" Frank asked.

"The detective will fill you in," she said in a casual, matter-of-fact voice.

I doubted it, but I knew in short order we would know most of what happened. Word gets out. She looked over at her partner, noticing he hadn't finished with the other three.

"Where are you all from?" she asked.

"All over," I said.

"We come here every year. There's sixteen of us," Frank said. "Well, some are fillers," he grinned and nodded at me.

I met and became friends with Frank in Spain, but hadn't had any additional personal contact with him until the prior golf trip. I had gotten to know him a lot better in the short span of time I'd been with him on these golf outings. I liked him.

"I'm from New Mexico, and Frank's from Texas," I said.

"The wild west," she said, smiling more with her eyes than

her mouth.

"Strong, I'm done here," Whip said.

"Okay," she took a couple steps away from us and called someone on her phone.

"Is that it?" Pete asked.

Officer Strong put her phone back in its holder on her belt. "Please, go eat your dinner but stay close to the hotel tonight. One of the detectives will want to talk to you this evening."

A couple of the guys said okay, and all of us went back into the restaurant. Covid numbers had fallen, and everyone in the group had gotten their vaccinations, but the concerns were still out there among the general public. Most of the restaurants still limited occupancy, and only a handful of other customers had chosen Waffles and Shakes for their dining experience. Of course, that could also be because the place resembled a larger than normal Waffle House and may not have made it to the top of the list of places to eat in Myrtle Beach.

"Should one of us call his wife?" Tom said.

"The police have a procedure to do that, and we couldn't answer any of her questions," I said.

"It would be best to call her tomorrow," Frank said.

"Once she hears, she may reach out to us. I know she has Vince's phone number. The four of them have been close," Mike said.

"Let's keep those rumors to ourselves," Tom said. He looked at me, knowing I had no idea about any rumors. "The four of them used to do a lot of traveling together. The next thing you know people are saying things."

"Enough said," I said and raised the palms of my hands up, facing Tom.

"You know their natural inclination is to think one of us, not only the five of us, but also the larger group, did it," Pete said.

"That's crazy, we just got here yesterday," Tom said.

We all ordered some variety of waffle and some flavor of a milkshake and ate our dinner during bouts of silence interrupted by remarks about how terrible this was. I got the impression that everyone was looking forward to their interviews with the detectives later that evening.

If they were guilty, they might show some signs of nervousness, and I saw none. That I went through this little mental analysis immediately bothered me. I had no role in the investigation and no reason to suspect anyone. Why then had I already started looking for 'tells', the little signs that might lead to the killer?

I told myself to leave it alone. I needed to focus on my golf and leave the investigation to the police. My golf today was almost embarrassing. I needed to play better and keep my nose out of the case. Unfortunately, deep down I knew both would be difficult things for me to do.

Chapter 4

Detective Barry Nichols recorded his entire interview of me on a small handheld device he referred to as modern technology that allowed him to capture everything I said. I felt like telling him recording devices had been around since before I was born, but I couldn't tell if he was being serious or not.

"After the round today, I had lunch with most of the other players at the course. A few usually skip lunch, but I don't know for sure if anyone did today," I said.

"Was Doug there?" Nichols asked.

"Yes, I believe so."

"Did you see him after you left the course?"

"No."

"That unusual?"

"No. I rarely see any of the players after lunch or before the five o'clock meeting other than my roommate."

"I thought the meeting today started at five thirty."

"It does, sometimes," I said. "Actually, the time for the meeting bounces around so much between five and five thirty, I never know myself."

"Who had a reason to kill Doug?"

"I have no idea. None at all."

Detective Nichols stared at me for a long second. "Tell me about the others in your group."

"I'm only a part time member. This is only my second time with them. We're all retired air force, but they're all pilots."

"Meaning?"

"I wasn't."

"Does that cause any friction?"

"None at all."

Nichols stared at me again, like he was either pondering a tough question or waiting for me to say something else.

"Anyone in the group have a reason to hurt Doug?" He asked, repeating his earlier question.

"You mean his attacker may not have meant to kill him?"

"That is always a possibility."

I knew that wasn't always true. People don't shoot someone in the head or stab them in the chest unless they meant to kill, but I understood him.

"I didn't know Doug well. The only contact I have ever had with him was on this and my last trip here, which was a couple years ago. He seemed like a nice enough guy. I haven't played in his foursome this year."

"What do you mean?"

"Each day we rotate players, so we get to play with just about everyone throughout the week. So far this week, we haven't been in the same foursome."

"Okay, tell me about Frank Derby."

"I met him in Spain over twenty years ago. We were assigned there along with Tom Marido and Pete Young. We all lived close together in the base housing, played some golf together, and became friends. I've run into them on a couple of occasions since then. I know of no issues that any of the three might have had with Doug."

"And Mike Powers?"

"Also at dinner with us tonight. I knew him slightly at the Air

Force Academy. We had a couple classes together, but until my first time joining this group in their golf trip here, I hadn't seen him since graduation. He seems like a nice guy and like the others, I have no idea what his relationship was with Doug."

"What about the guys who didn't go to dinner with you tonight?"

"Not uncommon, we only have two large group dinners."

"Anyone wonder off to see local friends?"

"I don't know. It's possible. I've never kept track of any of them."

"How about you? Any local contacts? You're not married? No local girlfriend?"

"No. I was married for a long time. Chasing women was a skill I lost years ago, if I ever had it. Here I play golf, socialize with the guys a little, and go to bed."

"No poker at night?"

"Not that I've seen."

"Okay, let's talk about the others."

"Other than their skill on the golf course or maybe their eating and drinking habits, I know very little. I'm not sure I could even tell you who's married or not," I said.

"Eric Gamble?"

"Might be the best golfer in the group. Lives in Florida."

"Jim McClennen?"

"Also from Florida, real nice guy, average golfer," I said.

"Skip the golf rankings and tell me about their relationship with Nelson."

"Okay, I don't know anything about their background with Doug."

"Let's see," he referred to his list of names. "How about this guy LG Johnson?

"I can't see it. Another nice guy. I don't know of any issues he may have had with Doug."

"So, you can't help me with this?"

"Wish I could, but I can't come up with a motive," I said.

"Vince Flores, James Streelman, Larry Brown, Dick Leyes, Bob Bishop, Bill Sanchez, and Edward White."

"That's all of them. I doubt if I could've remembered all the names. You'll get a lot more information out of the others. They've known each other for years, and this is like the eighth or ninth year they've been doing this."

When Detective Nichols left my room, I felt relieved that he hadn't tried pushing me into being more of a help in the investigation. I guessed he hadn't checked into my background yet, or he might've. I didn't want to get involved in a case that had no bearing on me, and in which, I couldn't see how I could help. It wasn't only my ego that had me worrying about the police wanting my help. It was my past. I'd been drawn into more investigations than I ever wanted and still had the scars to prove it.

Chapter 5

"What do you think?" Tom asked me.

We shared a standard two room suite in the hotel. Detective Nichols interviewed him after me and had left.

"I don't know what to think. It couldn't be one of us," Tom said.

"I agree. It would be hard for one of us to have slipped away, located Doug, and killed him without being noticed."

"We only see each other a couple times a year at the most. Doug flies for AirExpress now, as does LG, but LG lives in Florida, and Doug lives, I mean lived, out in California." Tom said. "They're both pilots, but I've never heard that they have flown together. A couple of the others also fly with AirExpress, but the same thing goes."

"We could be guessing all night, but we don't even know when or where or how Doug was killed."

"Think we'll find out?"

"Yes. It may even be on the local news tonight."

It was. A young, attractive TV reporter for the local news filled us in at the beginning of the ten o'clock broadcast.

"A visiting golfer was brutally murdered this evening in the old practice area of the Spiderwood Golf Course. A little after six, two women found the man sprawled out in the sand next to a practice green. The practice area is about a quarter mile from the clubhouse and the newer practice area. The victim had been struck in the head."

A knock on our door interrupted our focus on the news. I answered it and was surprised to see Officer Whip Miller standing there.

"We need you both to show us your golf clubs, now."

His now came across like a drill sergeant talking to a new recruit.

"You need to work on your presentation," I said. "You're not a storm trooper."

He bristled at my remark, but I turned and shouted to Tom that we needed to go get our clubs.

"No, you need to come with me and show us your clubs. We have a team in the parking garage already." I could sense he wanted to say something more to me, but he didn't. Maybe I wasn't the only person who had told him to work on his attitude.

We went with him to the garage. Both Tom's and my clubs were in my car. Like me, Tom had driven to Myrtle Beach, and we had agreed we each would drive three times to the course of the day. On the seventh day, we would drive ourselves, and both head directly home after golf and lunch at the course. He would make it home by dinner. It would take me a long two days.

We passed four of our guys coming back from the parking garage. A couple of them gave us a nod, but no one spoke. I attributed that to the presence of Officer Miller. Once at my car, it took me a few seconds to untangle the two golf bags crammed into the Mustang's small trunk.

"Please leave them there and back away," Detective Nichols said. He had teamed up with two other policemen who wore lightweight windbreakers with the initials CSI prominently displayed. They inspected each club before telling us we could put them back in the car. Their bodies blocked my seeing what they were doing with the clubs.

"Don't you have to send them off to the lab or something?" Tom asked.

"Not yet," Nichols said. "Thank you for your cooperation."

We stuffed the golf bags back into the trunk and left.

"Well, at least we now know they think the murder weapon was a golf club," I said after we got back outside.

"If we had killed him, we could have simply wiped the club clean, and they wouldn't have seen anything. That seemed strange to me," Tom said.

"They might have been looking for a bent or damaged club. Although it would be foolish for the killer to have kept the murder weapon. Most likely it's now in one of the hundreds of creeks and swampy areas around here."

"I agree. What club would you have used?"

I thought his question was in bad taste to say the least, but I answered it. "Probably my four-iron hybrid."

"Not me. I can't hit anything with my irons. I'd use my driver."

That night I managed to read for a while and get to sleep without any more disruption. Little did I know then that it would be the last peaceful night I would have for a while.

Chapter 6

The next morning Tom and I walked next door for breakfast. I was surprised to find four of the guys waiting for us. All sixteen of us would normally eat breakfast at roughly the same time, but no one waited for others to show up before going inside. Breakfast was included in the price of the rooms, so we rarely skipped it.

"We wanted to talk to you," LG Johnson said as the six of us entered the restaurant. I never knew what the L or the G stood for. Everyone just called him LG.

I didn't have to ask him why. I knew they wanted me to give them some sage update or answers. They would be disappointed.

"So, what do you think?" Vince Flores said.

"I don't know any more than you. It appears Doug was killed on one of the practice areas at Spiderwood. I've never played that course, so I don't know where it is."

"It's close. We've played it a couple times," Tom said.

"Someone killed him with a golf club," Dick Leyes said.

"I think that's the assumption they are going with. It would explain their request to look at our clubs last night," I said.

"Why us?" LG asked. "Anyone could have done it."

"True, but the usual suspects are spouses, friends, or other people associated with the victim. His wife is not here, although I imagine they will be trying to find out where she was yesterday. If they know of no one he knew here other than us, then they will focus their investigation on us. It's the only path they have at the moment."

"That sucks. We're guilty because we know him," Eric Gamble said.

"Not guilty, they are trying to eliminate us as well as trying to find the killer. I'm sure they are trying to identify anyone else who may have been at the scene. Right now, we're all that they have to go on. For a while, we will all be under the microscope."

"Have they asked you to help?"

"No, LG, and I hope they don't," I said.

"They should," Eric said. "We all know about you. You're famous."

"Hardly," I said, silently cursing the internet.

Since my wife left me, I had tried my best to be left alone. The divorce devastated me, leaving me adrift in an ocean of self-pity. I retired from the air force and moved back to New Mexico. That had been nearly a decade ago, and my attempt to be left alone had been a failure. Somehow, and through no fault of my own, I had been sucked into a number of murder investigations throughout the Southwest. I had hoped driving all the way to the Atlantic coast would have put some distance between me and the curse that had followed me around.

Other than my golfing buddies, no one knew me here. I could hope for a nationwide internet blackout and for my friends to keep their mouths shut; however, I knew I'd have more luck getting my first hole in one. It wasn't that I wouldn't help the police if I knew something, but I didn't.

"Do you think it's one of us?" Eric asked.

"No. I know of no motive and depending on the time of the attack, we were all together at the meeting."

"That's right," Eric said.

"It couldn't have been one of us," LG said.

They all seemed satisfied. Most smiled or nodded their head. I didn't have the heart to tell them that being at the meeting only gave them an alibi for the time they were there, and we still didn't know the time of the assault.

"It had to be someone else," Tom said.

"He did get into an argument with another group of golfers yesterday," Eric said.

"Did you mention it to Detective Nichols?" I asked.

"Nichols didn't interview me. A guy named Young did. I guess he was a detective or a deputy."

"What was the argument about?" Tom asked.

"He sliced his shot into another fairway, and his ball hit the cart these other guys were driving. They didn't get hit, but they were pissed that he didn't yell fore to warn them," Eric said.

"Why didn't he?" LG asked.

"Doug said he never saw the cart until it drove past a row of trees, and by then, it was too late. He said they drove into his golf ball."

"Did you mention it to Detective Young?" I asked again.

"Of course. I told him they were really mad. Doug apologized, but they were still mad. The detective wanted to know if I knew these other golfers. I didn't, of course, but I thought I could recognize them again if I saw them."

"Seems a stretch that would lead to someone killing him," Vince said.

"It does, but to walk out to a person in open daylight and beat him to death isn't very rational either," I said.

"It's crazy," Tom said.

We finished our breakfast discussing more theories. The

group had taken a poll the night before to determine if we should continue playing. Ten of the guys said we should, as that would be what Doug would want us to do. Five of us, including me, abstained.

As this was our second golf day, I drove south to Pawley's Plantation. I'd never played it, but Tom said it was one of the better courses we play. I thought they were all pretty good.

"I think it might have been one of us," Tom said, catching me off guard.

"How come?"

"It seems improbable that some stranger did it, and if his wife hired an assassin, the guy wouldn't have killed him with a golf club."

"True. It would have been easier to kill him with a pistol and then toss the pistol into some swampy area."

"What professional hitman would say 'time for me to go on my assignment, now where is my five-iron?" Tom said.

"Good point, but which one of us? Not me, not you, that leaves thirteen."

"Thirteen, not a lucky number."

I wondered about that. If it was one of the others, twelve of them would be innocent, and number thirteen would be the guilty guy. My phone rang with the call displayed on the screen in my car. The caller ID indicated the call came from the MBPD. I touched the screen to accept the call.

"Mr. West, this is Detective Nichols. I need you to come into the station this morning. The address is –"

I interrupted him. "Detective, I'm down at Pawley's Island on the third hole. I won't be able to make it there until after lunch, but I will be there as soon as I can."

He made a noise like he was muttering to himself. "Okay, but no later, or I'll send someone out to pick you up."

"Thanks," I said.

"A white lie," Tom said after I ended the call.

"I think if I said I was driving to the course, he would have tried to insist I turn around. Being on the course gave me a little more latitude."

"What do you think he wants?"

"I'm afraid someone recommended me to them, or they saw something on the internet."

"You're going to help them, aren't you?" The grin on his face couldn't have been bigger if he had watched me hit my golf ball into a lake. He knew I dreaded being put in this position. "I'll buy you a hat that says 'Snitch'."

"Come on, give me a break."

"I'm playing with you. The truth is someone killed Doug. If it was one of us, that person needs to be identified, arrested, and prosecuted. If it takes your involvement, so be it."

"I know, but it's going to rub some of the guys the wrong way. Besides, what in the hell am I supposed to do that they can't."

"Miss a three-foot putt."

Chapter 7

I could say that my concern about seeing the police later in the day affected my golf, but picking my head up and trying to hit the ball too hard took most the blame. That and missing another three-foot putt. At least my playing poorly kept a smile on my cart mate's face. I had played with Jim McClennen once before and had beat him. He was an easy guy with whom to play, but he was extremely competitive. He also remembered the last time we played together. Usually the more competitive a person, the harder I found getting along with them, but Jim made it easy. He always came up with the most outlandish, unrealistic prizes for the victor.

Whenever we had a similar shot, say we both had a shot from greenside sand trap, he would say something like, "closest to the hole gets a free weekend in Honolulu with Paula Abdul," or "gets to move into the spare bedroom at Halle Barre's house." By the time we finished playing, he'd won all the awards, even the "champion of the free world" award. At least, I kept my score below a hundred.

At lunch I sat next to Tom. Jim joined us at the four-person table, but while he was still in line ordering lunch, Tom asked me, "Well, did you win the 'stuck on an island alone with Jennifer Lawrence' award?"

"I'd be way out of my league with any of his prizes. Can you imagine what his dreams must be like at night?"

"More exciting than mine," Tom said.

By the time Jim returned to the table, Pete, still wearing his Borden's cap, had joined us. The two had driven down together and asked us if we wanted to play another nine holes after lunch.

"Can't," I said.

"Oh, come on. You just had a bad round this morning," Jim said.

"He's been summoned to the police station," Tom said.

"So, they finally figured out they could use some help," Pete said. "Don't get mad, but I told them about you."

"They were bound to find out, but all that stuff is way overblown," I said.

"I don't know. Climbing down the outside of a cruise ship at sea to save a damsel in distress seems pretty impressive to me," Pete said.

"I didn't climb. I was forced over the balcony and dropped to the balcony below. I was scared to death and very fortunate I didn't die in the process."

"Did it all in his underwear, too," Pete said to the other guys. "Anyway, joking aside, what harm can it do if you help?"

I had a thousand ways things could go wrong. Instead of listing them, I bit into my chili dog, spilling some chili on my white shirt. That brought more smiles to everyone except me.

Pete and Jim convinced Tom to stick around. They would drive him back to the hotel after they finished another nine holes.

I swung by the hotel to change shirts before heading to the police station, knowing it was more of an attempt to stall the inevitable than to make a good appearance. I parked on a side road and walked into the station. After a few minutes wait, Officer Louise Strong came into the waiting area and asked me to follow her.

"I've been assigned to assist the detectives. We're short of personnel, and the killing of a tourist, especially a golfer, gets higher priority than a local."

She sounded cynical. "It's got to be good for your career," I said.

"Oh, it is." She dropped me off in front an empty interview room.

"You're not coming in with me?"

She met my smile with her own half smile. "No, I don't get to do the fun parts. Detective Nichols will be with you in a minute."

It turned out to be two minutes, but I would've given him five before walking out. He looked tired, and I imagined he'd been up most of the night. There's an old theory that you need to solve a murder in the first twenty-four to forty-eight hours, or your chances of solving it go remote. It's a skewed statistic, but I understood the need for speed.

"Can I call you Jim?

"Of course."

"I'm Barry." He didn't offer a hand to shake. This wasn't an introduction. He was setting the tone of our new relationship, which, of course, he could change at any moment.

"What can I do for you, Barry?"

"A couple of your buddies seem to think you can simply solve this case for us."

"They exaggerate. I have nowhere near the talent or resources your department has."

"I don't know. I checked the internet. Seems you're a legend already," he said. Neither his voice or his facial expression gave me the impression he believed anything he said.

"Please, you know as well as I that the internet isn't reputable."

"Agreed, but as my boss has pointed out, how can it hurt to ask you for a little help. You know these guys even though you are the outsider. If nothing else you can help us eliminate them as suspects."

"You think it was one of us?"

"I have no reason to think it was or wasn't. You all have tickets out of here in five days. It'll be hard to keep you here, so I need all the help I can get. Believe me, we are not focused solely on your group, but you can't do much for us with the locals. Besides, there was no robbery, which we might expect if the killer was from here. What's the motive?"

"Did you hear that he hit a golf ball that hit another group's cart?"

"Yes, and I could see it if the murder happened right there in a fit of anger. But several hours later the other group tracks him down on a different course?"

I agreed, so I didn't press the point.

"Anybody making accusations within the group?"

"No, not at all. Not even a hint of one, yet."

"Yet," Nichols repeated, staring silently at me for a good five seconds. "I'm not asking you to do any digging, just let me know what they say. They're bound to start talking to each other. Gossip and knowledge sometimes blend together, and they have to all be very curious."

"Five days may be too short of time to learn much," I said.

"I know, that's why we need to have a direct line. Look, I'm not asking you to search anyone's room or follow anyone around. Listen and talk to them. You're doing that already. What's the worst that can happen? They might not invite you back?"

"They may not come back after this."

"I can have someone meet briefly with you each night, and you can pass along anything that you might have learned that day. You can always phone in anything significant."

"How about I call you?"

"Sure, we need your help, Jim, but I'd rather not be here waiting for a phone call. Fifteen of our primary suspects will be gone at the end of the week."

I knew all this, and I wanted him to solve the case, but I loathed being sucked into another murder investigation. Whenever I got involved, there seemed to be a lot of collateral damage. Me usually included.

"I'll do what I can," I said.

"Okay. You have my number already. Call me this evening."

I said I would, and we left the interview room. Nichols escorted me out of the building.

Chapter 8

The five-thirty meeting lasted an hour. The longest I could remember. In the first fifteen minutes, we took care of discussing the day's golf. Doug's murder dominated the next forty-five minutes. A few of the guys had already been drinking hard. I knew most of them drank, but this was the first time I could remember that anyone had come to the meeting nearly drunk.

"It had to be one of us," Larry Brown said. He hadn't said anything at the meeting up to that point.

"That's BS," Bill Sanchez said.

"It had to be," Larry said. The booze had his eyes looking out of focus.

"Well, who then?" LG asked.

"I don't know. You should know," Larry pointed at me with an unsteady finger.

"How could I know?"

Tom came to my defense. "He's not clairvoyant."

"I think everyone here ought to be put on a lie detector," Larry said.

"Sober up, man. We're as shook over this as you are," James Streelman said.

"Are you going to look into it?" Bill asked me.

"I'm not sure what I can do. The police have asked me questions like they have asked you all. They called me in today wanting me to help, but I don't see what I can do. As far as I know, there are no witnesses, no motive, and a whole city full of suspects."

"But you're going to help," Larry said. He wanted confirmation. It wasn't a question, yet I couldn't tell from his voice if he was for or against my involvement.

"Of course, don't we all want this murder to be solved?"

Larry nodded, and I noticed most everyone nodding or saying yes. It wasn't until later that I wondered who hadn't nodded or said yes.

After the meeting, Tom, Frank, Pete, Mike, and I went to a nearby Italian restaurant for dinner. The meal was okay, but I have a bad habit of eating too much pasta. A habit that should be easily avoided, but I never could say give me a half portion of lasagna or no to a basket of bread sticks to accompany it.

Our conversation initially centered around our server, a young man with six earrings in his right ear and an eyebrow stud. We were too old to appreciate such things. Our comments about the female server at a nearby table were much more favorable. In the middle of the meal, the conversation turned south, as far as I was concerned.

"Do you want to interview everyone in the group?" Pete asked.

I didn't and told him so, but that only brought up more recommendations from the others. Frank suggested I search all the rooms. Mike went so far as to suggest I bug a couple of rooms. Luckily the conversation spiraled into the ridiculous and everyone started trying to outdo the others with dumb suggestions.

By the time I arrived back to my room, I figured it was too late to call Nichols. I hadn't wanted to anyway. So, when my phone rang it surprised me, and I thought it might have been him.

"Mr. West?" a somewhat muffled male voice asked.

"Yes."

"This is Detective Nichols, can you come down to your car right away. I need to talk to you for a second. You'll understand, we've developed something new."

"My car?"

"Yes."

"You can't tell me on the phone?"

"It's something I need to show you. I'll see you in a minute." The line went dead.

"Crap," I said.

"What's up?" Tom asked.

"Nichols wants to show me something."

"At the station?"

"No, he's in the parking garage."

I left the room thinking how strange it was that he hadn't simply parked in the street or come up to my room. I was parked on the second floor, so I took the stairs and walked directly to my car. In the poor garage lighting, I couldn't see anyone around my car.

"Detective Nichols! Barry!"

No one answered, and I began to wonder if this was a prank. My car looked fine. I stood in the empty parking spot next to my car, wondering what to do when I heard something behind me. I started to turn around when I saw the golf club. More as a reflex than anything else, I tilted my head and tried to duck as the club slammed into my forehead. I fell backwards onto the concrete floor. My vision became blurry, but I could tell my attacker wore all black and had on a dark ski mask. The club came down again as I rolled away, striking me on my shoulder. I rolled under the large pickup truck parked next to me just as the lights of a vehicle appeared at the end of the row. It drove toward me and slowed.

Looking around I couldn't see the feet of my attacker. I crawled out from under the pickup, causing the driver, of what I could now see was an SUV starting to enter the vacant spot, to hit his brakes.

"What the hell, man?" the driver shouted out his window. He stepped out of his vehicle, and any anger he might have had vanished when he saw my face. "What happened to you? Are you ok?"

I touched my face, confirming what I felt. Blood flowed out of a gash above my left eye. "I've been attacked. Can you call 911?"

"Already on it," his passenger, whom I hadn't noticed, shouted out his window.

"You better sit down," the driver said.

I did. "You shouldn't park here now anyways. Crime scene."

"An ambulance is coming, Jack. There's another spot over there," the passenger pointed across the row and down a little further. Jack jumped into the car.

I felt a little dizzy, and my head hurt, but I knew I'd survive.

After they parked the SUV. Jack and his passenger approached me. "We're supposed to wait here until the ambulance gets here."

"Sorry about that. Did you see anyone leaving as you drove up?"

"No," Jack said.

"I saw someone who was going that way," he pointed at a spot in the direction where they went to park. "Didn't pay any attention to him. Sorry. You don't know who it was?"

Both men were in their early twenties. They stared at me. I couldn't tell if they were fixated with my injury, or if they thought I might die at any minute. Taking my key fob from my pocket I unlocked the Mustang.

"There is a clean towel on the back seat. Can one of you get it for me?"

The passenger retrieved it and handed it to me.

"Thanks. I'm Jim West, what's your name?" I pressed the towel against my injured forehead, hoping to stop or at least slow the flow of blood.

"I'm Cory and this is Jack," he said.

An ambulance siren switched on nearby, causing me to think we were close to a substation.

"Sounds like it will be here in a second," Cory said.

"Are you here for the golf?" Jack said.

"Yes," I said, thinking Jack was trying to lighten the mood.

"We are, too. We're trying to qualify for the state amateur tournament," Jack said.

"You must be good."

"He is. I'm playing, because he wouldn't come without me," Cory said.

"Don't believe him. He plays to a two handicap."

"He's scratch and has a good chance to make it to the state tournament. I hope to caddy for him there."

"Cory, don't give up before the qualifier even starts."

"You both are a lot better than me," I said. Even in my best day, I never made it to a single digit handicap.

The ambulance siren went silent as it entered the parking garage. I saw the reflections of the flashing lights and was somewhat surprised when the first vehicle that pulled up was a

MBPD sedan. The ambulance arrived seconds later.

Officer Louise Strong climbed out of the police car. "Is that you Mr. West? What happened?"

I pulled the towel away. "Some guy attacked me with a seven iron, or some other golf club."

"Jeez," she said, leaning in close to look at the wound.

"Let us have a look," said a young man, who had emerged from the ambulance.

Strong stepped away and walked over to Jack and Cory.

"I'm Caleb. Besides the head injury, do you have any other injuries?"

"No, oh yeah, he hit me in the shoulder, too, but that's just sore."

Caleb looked at my shoulder for a second and then back at my forehead. A second man from the ambulance joined him; however, after a few seconds, he wondered back to the ambulance, leaving Caleb to take care of me.

"What did he hit you with?" Caleb said as his fingers pressed around the wound.

"A golf club, an iron of some sort. I didn't get a good look at him or the golf club. How bad is it?"

"My guess is not too bad, but we need to get you to a doctor and run some x-rays. Do you feel like you can stand?"

"Yes. I was a little dizzy for a few minutes, but I feel better now."

He took a hold under my left arm and helped me stand.

"I'm okay."

"Well, let's get you into the ambulance where we can stop that bleeding and take some vitals," Caleb said.

"Hang in there," Jack said as the two young men walked away.

Officer Strong walked with us to the ambulance, but stayed outside it while I got situated inside.

"Mr. West," she said.

"Please call me Jim."

"Jim, what can you tell me about the attack?"

"Very little. It came out of the blue. Oh, one thing, I received a call from someone saying he was Detective Nichols and wanted to meet me by my car. That's why I came over here."

"Nichols?"

"Yeah, I know, and the implications aren't good either."

For a second, I don't think she understood what I meant, but then her eyes indicated she did. The list of suspects had narrowed from the whole city of Myrtle Beach to our little group of golfers. Who else would've known my phone number and knew that Nichols had been talking to us? I guess I knew it all along, but still I found it disappointing.

"Can you describe your attacker? Better yet did you recognize him?"

"No. He came at me from behind. As you can see, it's rather dark in here at night. I heard, or maybe I sensed someone was there and started to turn when he hit me. I only got a glance at the golf club. I think it was a seven iron, but I'm not sure why I think that."

"You didn't see his face?"

"He was wearing a dark ski mask, dark clothes, dark gloves, too. My attention was on avoiding the golf club. I didn't have enough time to avoid the first blow. I fell, and he swung the club again. I rolled toward the pickup, but the club hit my shoulder. I'm sure he was going for my head again. I kept rolling and got under the pickup. Just then, Jack and Cory drove up onto this level, and their headlights scared off the guy."

"Why would he attack you?"

"Good question?" I said, although I knew the answer.

"Louise, you want to follow us or wait 'til someone else gets here?" Caleb asked.

"I need to wait here. It shouldn't be long, Jim, then I'll join back up with you at the hospital. I have a few more questions."

Chapter 9

Other than the aggravation of my wound being poked, scrubbed and stitched, the ride to and my time at the hospital proved uneventful. Officer Strong showed up while I was sitting alone in a room, waiting to be released.

"I hope you didn't take you shirt off just for me," she grinned.

"And I hope you're here to drive me back to the hotel." For some silly reason, I felt a little self-conscious, sitting there shirtless.

"I take it this wasn't on your car when you parked it," she held up her phone to show a picture of a blood splatter that ran up the passenger side window.

"No. Too bad that's not my assailant's blood."

"We've got a team going over the area right now. If he left any trace behind, we'll get him. We're also talking to everyone right now. Have you thought about what you are going to do?"

"What do you mean?" I asked.

"Are you going to continue to golf?"

"Yes. This will give me better excuses for my bad shots. The doctor said my shoulder is fine. It'll be sore for a few days, but that's all. My head injury shouldn't affect my game. In fact, it might help me keep my head still."

"Golfing in a group when your cart mate might be your attacker and a murderer seems to me to be a bit unnerving. Besides your eye is almost swollen shut. That has to bother you."

"I'll be fine. They said the swelling should go down a little overnight. The only thing I'm worried about is whether I can wear a hat. The older I get, the more the sun bothers my eyes."

"Are you sure you want to stay with the group? No one would blame you if you took a couple days off to give us time to catch the guy."

"I don't think he'll try anything again. He's got to be shook. Have you checked to see if anyone in the group has disappeared?"

"All still there, and unfortunately, security cameras have given us zip. Most have been damaged by vandals and never repaired."

A nurse came in, and Louise walked around behind me. The nurse looked more tired than I felt. Her dark brown hair pulled tight behind her head.

"Mr. West, you can go. Follow the instructions on the sheet of paper we gave you. We've already scheduled a brief follow-up for Friday afternoon. Keep this with the other papers." She handed me an appointment slip.

"Thanks, I appreciate your looking after me," I said.

She gave me a tired smile. "I wish everyone was as easy as you." She nodded at Louise and left the room.

"Ready? I brought you a clean shirt?" She took a grey, collarless tee shirt, out of the small paper bag she was carrying.

"Thanks. You all can keep the bloody one when you're done with it." I winced as I pulled the shirt over my head. It was a little large on me.

"It belongs to Whip. He leaves a couple spares in the car. He'll never miss it. Come on," she walked out of the room, and after scooping up the papers on the desk, I followed her.

"My car is over there by the diner," she pointed to a spot two blocks away.

The cool breeze off the ocean felt good, but an odor from some trash containers in an alley next to the hospital ruined the night's ambience.

"Yuck," I said, and Louise scrunched her nose in agreement.

As we approached her car, Louise said, "Can I buy you a cup of coffee? I know it's late, but I'd like to ask you a few more things."

The lights were on in the diner and an older couple sat inside at a table next to the window. A handwritten sign on the window declared the place stayed open until midnight.

"Sure."

"Officer Strong, how are you tonight?" A tall, thin man in an apron, greeted us. He looked to be in his sixties, the hair on his head thinning and white, while his beard had a little grey in it and needed grooming. He carried a rag that he used to clean the table in the corner to our right.

"Crazy again, Phil. Got any coffee and cherry pie left?"

"If we don't, I'll bake a fresh one for you right now."

"Don't do that," she said, pointing at a table and lifting an eyebrow at me as if to ask if that one would be okay.

I nodded, and she led me to it. Phil had two cups and a pot of coffee at our table by the time we sat down. "Mister, I could've warned you about this police officer. She's got a mean left hook." His eyes were on my bandaged forehead.

"Don't scare him away, Phil. I only met him yesterday."

"Would you like a slice of pie, too?"

"Sure." I wasn't hungry, but when had that stopped me from eating cherry pie? "I guess you're a regular here," I said as Phil sauntered back to the counter.

"Been coming here since I joined the force, nearly twelve

years now. Phil's been here the whole time. Diner belongs to his family, and he manages it, I think. Thanks for letting me talk you into stopping here before I take you back."

"Well, tempting me with coffee and pie wasn't really fair."

"If you start not feeling well or just want to go back to your room to lie down, please tell me."

"No, I'm fine, and I'm sure when I get back, everyone will want to know what happened."

"Tom Marido stopped by at the hospital, but we shooed him away. Are you worried about going back to the hotel?"

"No, whoever did this is more worried now than me. I doubt if he'll try something else."

"Why did he attack you?"

"They have some inflated belief in my capabilities in solving murders. My guess is he was worried I would ferret him out. It's dumb, because I don't ferret, I stumble."

"Why do they think that about you?" she asked.

"Hyped up gossip and the internet. It's stupid." I didn't elaborate, and she left it alone.

"You were in the military. Is that where you got those scars?"

She must have seen them at the hospital when I had my shirt off. I hadn't thought about them at the time, being more concerned that I had let myself put on a little weight and had prematurely succumbed to the dreaded mid-century-of-life slouch.

"No, those are all from my failure to better manage my retirement. Like tonight. Think it'll scar?"

"Yes, sorry."

"So much about me, tell me about yourself. Are you from South Carolina?"

"Yes, spent almost all my life here. Only been to North Carolina and Virginia. Don't get me talking about it, because I'll only get depressed." She smiled as though she was joking, but I believed her comment held a kernel of truth.

"Did you grow up wanting to be a police officer?"

"I think I did, although it wasn't until I neared graduation from Central Carolina that I decided to join. Been a few times I've regretted it, but mostly it's been a good job. I have a good chance to make sergeant this summer."

"That's good," I said.

"How'd you like the military?"

"I enjoyed my career, probably too much."

"Why do you say that?"

"I think I gave it more attention than I should've, and my wife left me. Long story, but it's been years now." I didn't want to get into it.

The pie arrived with a small scoop of vanilla ice cream on top.

"Thanks, Phil." Louise said. She took a bite of pie.

The warm pie had softened the ice cream. A little liquid stream of vanilla ice cream ran down the side of my pie and onto the plate. I maneuvered my fork to get a little ice cream along with some pie.

"Delicious," I said to Phil. He leaned against the counter a few feet away, watching us.

"Who do you think we can eliminate?" Louise asked.

"What do you mean?

"You must have some sense of height. Even if you only saw your attacker briefly, were you looking up at him or down?"

"I've thought about that. It's not that simple, because I never really looked at him. However, I think we can exclude Jim

McClennen and LG Johnson because they're at least six-five, and maybe Frank Derby because he's five-nine. But even then, if the tall guys crouched a little when they swung, they would look shorter, and I guess if I ducked more than I thought, Frank would look taller."

"True, but it allows us to prioritize our investigation to look at the others first. Brings down our primary suspect pool to eleven," she said.

"I can't believe it's Tom, either.

"Why?"

"He was with me when I received the phone call that supposedly came from Nichols, so he could only be an accomplice."

"Let's hope we don't have two or more of them working together. By the way, we're looking at everyone's golf clubs again. I understand you don't keep track of how many clubs each of you use?"

"No," I said. "There's a maximum number that's allowed, but we don't enforce it. Most of us carry a few less anyway. No one would notice if one of us started the week with fifteen clubs and ended with thirteen."

"I may have asked you before, but do you feel the need for any protection?"

"No. I'll stay much more alert from now on."

"We'll want a written statement tomorrow. Will that be a problem?"

"No. I can come in after lunch."

"Are you sure you want to play golf tomorrow?"

"Yes. I want to, and I think it will ratchet up the stress on the guy who attacked me. I might notice something."

"Well, stay with the group. Wander off on your own, and you will make yourself a target again. You know, you'll likely have a whopper of a headache."

"Something else I can blame my poor golf on. One can't ever have enough excuses when it comes to golf."

She had a nice smile. Her phone buzzed. She looked at it, texting a message in response.

"Am I keeping you from a date?" I asked.

"Ha! That was only Nichols wanting to know if I've learned anything new."

"Sorry I haven't been more help."

"I don't think anyone expected you to have seen much. Barry said as much while he was at the crime scene. Too dark, assailant wearing dark clothes and a mask, attack from behind with blows to the head. It's a scenario we see too often. A favorite of the intelligent mugger. However, we're giving the scene a serious forensic going over, and that may be our best bet to catch the guy. People often leave some trace behind."

I nodded, knowing what she said was true. Cases have been solved with the discovery of one strand of hair.

"The state boys are even here to help. The golfing tourism business always brings out the first team."

"You mentioned that before. It's a sore spot?"

"Yes. I would never be involved as much in the investigation if this was a local killing. It's like there are two different priorities. I believe we have too many unsolved local cases, because we didn't go all out early in the investigation. They didn't rate the extra effort."

"Unfortunately, I think that happens everywhere. A homeless person gets murdered in a big city, and unless it's one in a series of similar murders, it gets stuck so far on the back burner, virtually nothing gets done about it. A sad reality of priorities, politics, and workload."

"Believe me, I know. I've even been cautioned away from a couple when I tried to put a little overtime in an effort to develop some evidence. They tell me to let the detectives do it, for me to do my own job, but nobody does anything."

I guessed at least one such case had bothered her a lot, but I didn't pry, and she didn't elaborate.

"I'll get off my soapbox. I shouldn't be discussing it with you, and I want you to know I'm happy to be included in this investigation. So please don't go telling Detective Nichols that I don't want to be involved."

"There's no reason I would, Officer Strong," I said. "Why would I sacrifice my chance to get another piece of pie?"

"Please call me Louise."

I changed the topic to hurricanes, fires, and flooding. All issues I knew have periodically affected the area and, more importantly, had nothing to do with police work.

Chapter 10

"So, what's she like on a date?" Tom ribbed me.

I had told him about my pie and ice cream with Officer Strong. After his initial questions about the attack, I knew the topic would get his attention.

"She's nice, but that was hardly a date," I said.

"You're single. I know you have a relationship, but you're still single and across the state line. I'd try to capitalize on this. Keep everything off social media. Keep me informed, and I'll coach you through this."

"Ha! Some help you'd be."

"You think she has something going on with the other cop?" Tom asked.

"Whip? I doubt it."

"Kind of a cool name, and they both work out. You never know."

"Cool name? I wouldn't be surprised if he didn't give it to himself. She doesn't seem to be all that impressed with him," I said.

"That's good. She may have a thing for old, I mean older men." Tom had a hard time keeping a straight face. "She married?"

"No. She doesn't wear a ring and didn't give me any indication she was."

"Well, I would do the same thing if I was trying to pick up a woman. Ditch the ring and act like I'm single." He was loving this.

"I may not see her again, so it doesn't really matter."

"Did she give you her number?"

"I have her card."

"When you call her, see if she has a hot friend. We could double date."

"Double date? When was the last time you double dated?"

"Damn! You got me there. I can't remember. In college for sure, but that's too far back for me to remember. After I got married, we've been out with other couples. Does that qualify as double dating?"

"It could."

"No, no, that's not at all what I had in mind," he said.

"You mean that's not what you imagined in your little, dirty mind."

"It's not that little," he said, grinning.

"Well, I don't see dating or double dating in our future this week."

"That's too bad. She's ripped. Her muscles have muscles, but in a good way. Think you can talk her into going swimming with us in the ocean?"

"Did you even bring a swimming suit?" I asked.

"No, but I'll buy one. Did you tell her you were OSI?" Tom asked, referring to my years with the Air Force Office of Special Investigations.

"No."

"You should. Tell her I was Special Ops."

"You were in Special Ops?"

"No, but we only have four days left. Too little time to be honest and get anywhere."

"You always have next year, Tom."

"That's true. I could set the foundation this year. Don't tell her I'm with Special Ops. Tell her I work with the homeless and travel back and forth to Africa to help feed the children."

"Sounds like a plan." I didn't think I'd be coming back next year.

"What impresses me is that she obviously lifts weights, but everything is in good proportion. It's like she has more curves to her body. A lot of women who lift weights and go in for body building end up looking wrong. She's done it right."

"I agree."

"I mean I can live with stick figure legs and arms, that seems to be the fashion, but she's done it right."

I didn't say I agree again. The conversation had started to become tedious.

"I'm having another beer, you want one?" he asked.

"Okay." With the pain meds they gave me at the hospital, I figured the beer would knock me out, and I was ready to go to sleep.

He returned from the refrigerator with two Yuenglings. We talked about the golf course we'd be playing next and how everyone was playing this year. Gratefully, he didn't bring up Louise again.

At breakfast the next morning, Bill Sanchez approached me in the buffet line and asked if I could sit with him. He had something he wanted to tell me. Tom and I had walked over together, but when Bill indicated a table with only two chairs and one already taken, Tom told me he would join Vince and Larry. I felt like telling Bill no, but I followed him to his table.

"Thanks, Jim. I hope you don't mind but this has been bothering me."

"Something I did? I asked.

At first, Bill thought I was serious, then he smiled. "No, no, not about you, well I guess it is in a way." His eyes went to my bandaged forehead.

"It's about Eric and Bob, but listen, please don't let them know I'm telling you this. Most the guys know anyway, but I'd rather they not know it came from me."

"Okay, what is it?"

"Eric, Bob and Doug had a business together for several years. It started when they were still on active duty. It was more of an investment in real estate than a business like a company. They pooled some of their money together and bought up some foreclosures in the Sacramento area. Doug had the lead role because he lived out there, but I believe they were equal partners financially."

"Houses?"

"Yes. They spent some money to make them presentable, not perfect, and resell them. Sometimes, if the buyer couldn't get credit, they would hold the note. They had to foreclose on one or two of their own buyers. That's not the point though," Bill said.

"Okay."

"Everything went well for a while. Then, last year, Doug decided to close everything down and split the profits. Both Eric and Bob were upset about it, because Doug just up and closed it down. Last year here at the golf week, there was a lot of arguing and animosity among the three. They had always been the best of friends before."

"Legally, could he do it?"

"Yes. He had set it up where any of them could pull out and dissolve the relationship whenever they wanted."

"That seems okay," I said.

"It did to everyone at the time. However, he shut down the business without telling or getting the other two involved. He said he sent them an email, but I never saw it, not that I should've. The bigger problem was that Eric and Bob believed they should've made more money from the split. While as far as I know, they never came out and publicly accused Doug of cheating them, but that's what we all understood."

"How much money are we talking about?"

"I don't know for sure, but I got the feeling last year it was tens of thousands. If Doug had gotten killed last year, I think everyone would have put them at the top of the suspect pool," Bill said.

"That's a good point, but a year has passed. How were they getting along this year? Not knowing the background, I hadn't been paying any attention."

"The old friendship wasn't there, but to be honest, I hadn't noticed any outward hostility. Doug had a brand-new set of Calloway clubs. I did notice that. If they saw the clubs, they may have wondered if he bought them with their money."

That was a stretch. Any of the group could afford a new set of clubs without breaking the bank. I couldn't see the new clubs sending anyone into a killing rage.

"Who knows Eric and Bob the best?"

"The best? I don't know. We all know them. Maybe Ed, you want me to tell him you want to talk to him?"

"No, it might be best for you to keep a low profile."

"Good point. I'm going back for more bacon. Wants some?"

While Bill made little dashes into and out of the buffet line, grabbing some bacon and some more grits, I looked around the dining area. Life appeared to be moving along as usual for the dozens of golfers taking advantage of the breakfast which was included with the golfing package and staying at the hotel. The volume in the room during breakfast was loud, and the conversations usually centered around yesterday's experiences or the expectations the golfers had for today. Some in our group might still be focused at Doug's murder, but for most in the room, it was something that might as well have happened on the moon. I wondered if that was a good thing, or if their apathy was one of the reasons less is done about violent crime.

"How do you think you'll play today?" Bill asked when he returned to the table.

Chapter 11

By chance, Eric Gamble and I were in the same foursome that day. He rode in the other cart with Dick Leyes, but I had plenty of time to talk to him. The whole foursome seemed to be in a morose mood. Doug's death must have finally set in, I thought, as the group had been in disbelief the day before.

On the third hole, a slight dog leg left, Eric and I were looking for our golf balls in the right rough. My cart partner, Larry Brown, and Dick were searching along the bank of a small pond on the left side of the fairway. Sadly, not one of us hit our drives onto the wide expanse of green grass known as the fairway.

"I know everyone is talking about Bob and me," Eric said.

"I heard something about a business deal that fell apart. Is that what you're talking about?" I feigned ignorance which wasn't too hard. Relieved that he brought up the subject, I wanted him to keep talking.

"Yes. It came to a head last year while we were all together. You weren't here, right?"

"No, I didn't come last year. What happened?"

"Bob and I had been investing in a real estate business with Doug. The three of us had known each other since pilot training. The ass up and sold everything without telling us or otherwise getting us involved. We got a letter and a check about a month before the trip here last year."

"I could see how that would irritate you."

"It wasn't that. All the paperwork, past estimates of the

business value, etc. indicated the value of our holdings amounted to significantly more than what we got paid."

"How did he explain that?"

"Expenses. Legal fees, real estate fees, repairs, staging costs, taxes, etc., etc. You name it, he included it as a cost that ate away at our profits."

"Did you lose money?"

"That's just it. We didn't, but we only made pennies on the dollar to what both Bob and I believed we should have made. We contemplated suing, but a lawyer we talked to said without hard evidence and the fact that we made a profit, our chances were slim. If we recovered any more from him, it would likely only go to pay any legal costs we incurred in the process."

"You argued about it last year while you were here," I said.

"Yes, and it got heated. You know, real estate transactions are a matter of public record. We saw how much he sold the houses for. If we were going to kill him, we would have done it last year."

"Did you make money off the business each year?"

"Yes, we each received a quarterly check, but we put some of that back into the business, too. Oh, here's a ball. I think it's mine. What were you playing?"

"A yellow Bridgestone."

"Nope this is white, must be mine." He started preparing for his shot.

I found mine a few seconds later, barely visible in the thick grass. We both managed to hit our balls onto the fairway near the green and hadn't walked very far before the two carts came to pick us up. The topic of conversation changed to the large alligator the other guys had seen near the pond.

Built on thousands of acres of wet coastal plains, many of the courses in the Myrtle Beach area included a wide selection of wildlife. Alligators, snakes, and turtles had lived in the area before man had ever settled there.

There was a small lake behind the green, and as I stood on the green waiting for Dick to putt, I saw two small alligators sunning themselves on the bank of the lake. I also saw a turtle balanced on top of a wooden post that rose vertically out of the water for about eight inches. The post was a couple of feet away from the shoreline. I had no idea how the turtle got there, but I remembered seeing one atop a similar post before on one of the other courses we played. Most of the courses had similar small lakes or ponds. Too many, in fact, as far as my golf was concerned. The thought came to mind that the police would never find the golf club or clubs used in the attack on Doug and me.

Eric only made one other comment to me that morning about Doug's death. In a rare stroke of luck, the two of us had hit our drive on the short par three thirteenth hole onto the green. The other two were in the weeds to the right of the green and were discussing the propriety of taking a free drop.

"You can write me off your list," Eric said.

"My list? I don't have a list."

"You know what I mean. I honestly did not kill Doug. I didn't hate him. I don't know who did, and, by the way, I didn't do that to you either." His eyes looked at my bandage before he turned his head to watch Dick hit his ball onto the green.

As we drove to the next hole, Larry said, "We were both near some roots, so we both took a free drop."

The group had a formal set of rules, which did find its basis in the actual rules of golf. Our rules, however, included a number of asterisks to accommodate faster play and in recognition that none of us were heading to the PGA tour anytime soon. I actually liked it. There is nothing more welcome to a golfer's ear than, "That's good." Most of us would loiter over a three-foot putt, waiting and hoping for someone to take us out of our misery.

Someone made another wise decision during the first few years of the group's existence to modify the rules, allowing our players to drop the ball on the other side of the water if, by some fallacy in course design, we hit our first shot into a body of water situated in front of the tee box. Even I agreed this modification to the rules expedited speed of play and saved us from hitting several balls into the same body of water.

On the seventeenth hole, both Larry and I hit our balls near each other in the fairway. We sat in the cart waiting for the group ahead of us to get off the green. Eric and Dick had parked in the shade in the left rough.

"Larry, Eric mentioned that he and Bob had a falling out with Doug over some business they were in. Do you think Doug ripped them off?"

"You mean, do you think he or Bob could have killed Doug?"

"He brought it up. Don't get mad at me. He wanted me to know about it and wanted me to know that he didn't kill Doug or attack me."

"No, I don't think he or anyone else in our group killed Doug. None of us are perfect."

"No one is," I said.

"You know, even your pal Tom is not so innocent."

"Why?"

"He's the only one among us that I know of who has been in a real fist fight."

"I know the story."

"Well, then you can stop looking at me."

"I'm not looking at anybody, not you, not anyone. The police are doing the looking, not me," I said.

"But you're pointing the fingers. That's what you guys always did."

"Not this time."

Larry shook his head like he didn't believe a word I said and walked away.

I knew all about Tom's fight. We were both young when we met, and the fight occurred before that. Tom and a lot of other junior officers were at the Officers Club on some air force base. Everyone had been drinking too much, a regular Friday night occurrence back then. Something happened, it didn't have to be much, and Tom got into it with another young officer. The fight didn't last long, despite half the crowd cheering them on.

Tom's career almost came to an end that night, but the government had invested a ton of money turning him into a fighter pilot. The generals didn't want to throw that money away. That and the fact that no one could remember who started the fight saved his career.

Larry's reaction to our conversation seemed a little strong, and I wondered why. While I had come to the conclusion that Doug's murder had to be someone in the group, I didn't press him.

Chapter 12

Detective Nichols looked at my statement and then asked me. "Are you sure this is all you want to say?"

"What do you mean? It's everything that happened, from the phone call to the ambulance arrival."

"But you can't describe your assailant any better?"

"Like I said, my attention was on the club. If I could describe him any better, believe me, I would."

"And no one in the group has told you who they think attacked you?"

"No. Is there a reason why you think I wouldn't tell you if someone mentioned a name to me?"

"Misplaced loyalty, fear, maybe you want to take care of your attacker by yourself."

"Trust me, that's everything I can remember about last night, and no one has given me the slightest hint that they know who attacked me."

"So be it. West, do I need to remind you that you're not in New Mexico? The police run the investigations here. If you hear anything, you need to let us know immediately."

I should have mentioned something about the dispute Eric and Bob had with Doug the year before, but Nichols had irritated me. Upon leaving Nichols small office, I noticed two South Carolina State Policemen waiting outside his office with Detective Young. Both looked at me with interest as I walked by.

Back at the hotel, I showered and took a nap before the

afternoon meeting, hoping to shake a lingering headache. After the meeting, I would try to get Bob to talk to me about the business fallout with Doug. I found it interesting that Eric had adamantly claimed he didn't kill Doug, but he didn't defend Bob.

As it turned out, I didn't need to approach Bob, he came up to me as the meeting ended and asked if he could talk to me privately.

"Sure. Where?" I asked.

"Across the street at Starbucks in fifteen minutes. Is that good?"

"I'll be there."

Bob left the room, while I stayed and talked to Mike, Frank, and Tom about dinner plans.

"Dick and LG want to join us tonight and suggested Mexican. You know that place we usually go to," Tom said.

I didn't know the restaurant, but the rest did and agreed. They set a time to leave the hotel, giving me forty minutes to talk to Bob and get back.

Walking back to our room, Tom said, "More bodyguards for you this way."

"What do you mean?"

"We all talked. Pete, too, but he had to make a phone call after the meeting. We think someone needs to be with you from now on. Whoever it was may want to finish the job."

"I appreciate it, but it's not necessary. Right now, I need to go talk to Bishop. He asked me to meet him at Starbucks. He wanted me to come alone."

"Bob? I bet it's on that fallout from last year. I can't see him doing it. He's never really struck me as being very brave. Keep that between the two of us, but he's awful timid."

"Still, I need to go."

"Okay, I can watch Starbucks from here. It's daylight, so as long as you don't go out the back door, I can see you going and coming."

I grinned. They were going to take this seriously. "Fine. I won't be long."

He took the up elevator, and I went down. Crossing the street, I arrived a few minutes early but found Bob already there. I hadn't considered him as being meek, but looking at him, I could see how someone might. Slender with hair already thinning, he did kind of look like the exact opposite of Whip. Yet I knew that enough anger and a weapon could overcome "meekness".

I remembered a situation where a petite mother, described by everyone as shy and very nice, defended her eleven-year-old son and herself from three older, bigger, teenage boys. They were trying to take her son's backpack, and when he resisted, they began hitting and kicking him. She flew out of the house grabbing a plastic baseball ball bat and proceeded to go through the teenagers like Attila went through the Romans.

Of course, she was a mother defending her son, and Bob had nothing similar to drive him into attacking me.

"Here," Bob called when he saw me.

"Hey, Bob, what's up?"

"Want something?" he asked, ignoring my question.

"No, I'm good, but thanks."

He looked around for a minute like he wanted to make sure no one could hear him. The place didn't have any other customers.

"Eric said he talked to you."

"Yes, he did."

"What did he say?"

"He briefly told me about how you and he felt like Doug had cheated you."

"We didn't just feel like it, he did cheat us. I've gone over everything a million times, and we should have received at least five times the amount we got. Probably ten times, if you want to know the truth."

"Okay. You confronted him last year."

"Yes, but we had already been in touch with him. Between emails and phone calls, I made my point several times before the golf trip."

"Yet he still came."

"Yes. Doug is a smooth talker. Everyone likes him, but I finally saw him for what he was. A snake, a slithery bastard of a snake. How can eighty percent of the gross profits get eaten up by expenses? It's not possible. The guy was shrewd, and he screwed us."

"What happened last year?"

"He came with all this paperwork. He wanted to show it to everyone, not just us, to prove his innocence. If I was going to kill him, it would have been last year. I didn't do it, and I certainly had no reason to attack you. By the way, how are you?"

"I'm good, only a bruised forehead and some stitches. I even played my best game of golf so far this week."

He grinned. "That's crazy how that works, but you need to know I didn't kill Doug, and I'm sure Eric didn't either."

"I believe you," I said to mollify him. "Who do you think did it?"

"No idea, but you ought to talk to the guys who fly AirExpress with him. Rumors have it that Doug may have had an affair in Brazil."

"How could his having an affair get him killed?"

Bob looked at me, and for a moment, I thought he wasn't going to answer. "Maybe he wasn't the only one. I don't want to say any more about it, but you might find a better motive there."

"Ok," I said, already tired of this cryptic conversation. "You know this business stuff will be discovered by the police, if it hasn't already. Apparently, everyone knew about it."

"I'm kind of surprised they haven't asked me about it yet."

"I'm sure they will. LG is with AirExpress. Who else is?"

"Streelman. Don't tell him I told you, but everyone knows anyway. He hasn't been with them long, maybe a year or a little more. Maybe two years, I can't remember anything anymore."

"I still don't see how having an affair can cause his death unless you're telling me Doug's wife hired someone."

"That may be what happened, but you need to talk to those two. You know, I can't see any of us doing it."

"Why?"

"Because we are all friends. We served together. You know, we're like brothers-in-arms, all that stuff. We would die for each other. Why would we kill each other?"

"The attack on me would tend to indicate otherwise. I can't explain that away."

"I can't see it. Even after what he did to me and Eric, I can't see it. You got attacked by some mugger. Had nothing to do with Doug's death. Had to be."

I actually admired his attitude, if he was being truthful. Yet I knew, whether he wanted to believe it or not, that servicemen and women do kill each other. Not at the rate as those outside the service, I thought, but they still did. Petty jealousies, envy, and greed existed. Then there were those who were just plain evil.

"I gotta run. Sorry about your head," Bob said, standing up and walking out the Starbucks.

I sat there for a few seconds after he left. What a strange discussion, I thought, wondering if he knew more, or if he was trying to take the focus off him by telling me about affairs in South America. I'd have to ask Tom about it later, but first there was a Mexican dinner to enjoy.

Of course, Tom didn't let me wait to tell him what happened. Even before we reached his car for the short drive to the restaurant, he was grilling me.

"So, what happened? What did he say?"

"The same as Eric. He didn't kill Doug, but he was still mad at him for cheating him out of his fair share. He said Doug brought paperwork with him last year to show everyone."

"He did, but I didn't look at it. I didn't want to take sides. These guys are all friends of mine. Last year no one died, and if someone had cheated another, then that was between them. This year is different. This golf trip won't happen again if the killer isn't caught. Some of the guys are talking about going home early this week. One or two might've left already if it wasn't for the police telling them they had to stick around."

"That's understandable."

"Do you think Bob could've done it? He's a skinny little guy. Hits the ball a long way, though."

"In my mind the guy who attacked me was bigger," I said.

"Yeah, it won't do your secret agent image any good to be taken out by a skinny little guy like Bob."

Chapter 13

My enchiladas verde were pretty good, and considering I've spent my last decade back on the New Mexico – Texas border, I know my Mexican food. Like a true New Mexican, I won't even argue with a Californian who has a misguided belief that the best Mexican food can be found out there.

The conversation at dinner had a hard time getting off how I felt, who did I think attacked me, and what the police were doing about it. LG did most of the asking which made me a little suspicious, since only minutes earlier, Bob had fingered him as someone to suspect.

My phone buzzed in my pocket a few minutes before we left the restaurant. The text read, "Can I buy you another piece of pie? It's important, L."

I wasn't hungry. Munching on chips and salsa fills up the gaps between a platter of enchiladas, beans, and rice. However, she said it was important, and she was my only ally on the force. I sent her an affirmative response, received a text from her saying twenty minutes, and responded that I may be a few minutes late.

"Everything okay?" Tom asked after we left the restaurant and approached his car.

"Yeah, Louise wants to see me again tonight."

He grinned from ear to ear. "You lucky dog. If she shows up in civilian clothes, she wants to take you home. Don't blow it."

"She wants to talk about the investigation. Sounds like she may have something new."

"Something new for you, I bet. Remember I want details and a referral please. We only have a few days left, and then I go back to the old battle ax."

"I'll do my best," I said. "It's a good thing I don't record these conversations and send them to your wife."

He laughed. "That might give me a motive to take a four-iron to your head." Looking embarrassed, he added, "You know I was just kidding about the four-iron comment."

"I know you were."

"Good, that was in bad taste, but seriously, a referral please," he said with a laugh, closing the door behind him.

He had parked a level above my car. Five minutes later, I arrived at the diner and found Louise standing at the counter talking to Phil. She was wearing her police uniform. Two other couples occupied tables by the windows facing the street.

"Long day?" I asked.

Phil took us to our same table. "Yes," he said.

"Same thing tonight?" Louise asked me.

"Sounds good."

Phil nodded and walked away.

"The question was for you. Looks like you've had a long day," I said.

"You don't look too sharp either. You've got food on your shirt."

I looked down and saw some salsa. "I didn't mean it that way. Here it is nearly eight o'clock, and you're still in uniform."

"Sorry. I shouldn't have snapped at you, but it's not been a good day."

"Well, then let me buy tonight."

"Okay. You should know they found out about you?"

"Found out? What?" Of course, for a moment my mind focused on the week's events, not my past.

"About all the stuff you've been involved in. The internet, you know."

"Most of that stuff is hyped up, besides Nichols knew it yesterday."

"Well, today, everyone knows about you. Now they're arguing whether you'll try to solve this without sharing, thereby screw up our investigation, or if we should make you an official consultant for the next few days. Either way, no one is a big fan of yours right now."

"Not even you?" I smiled.

"Don't push your luck," she said, but her face lightened up.

"You did ask me to come here tonight."

She looked at me without speaking. Phil brought our coffee and pie, set them down, and left us. I could tell her mind was trying to figure something out.

"It's not you, and I'm happy to be here right now," she said.

"Good, because I'd rather be talking to you than to Nichols."

"He's actually one of the good ones. Most of the guys back at the department are great, but there are a couple that are, well to keep it clean, jerks, big sexist jerks. Luckily, none of them are in my chain."

"Then you can ignore them."

"I do, but it's still tiresome. I'm here because I'm a good cop, I want to be involved with this investigation, and I already know you. Nichols needs someone to stay in close contact with you, and I told him I'd be happy to do it."

"Because I was assaulted, or because they think I might be trying to solve the case on my own?"

"All the above, plus even if you aren't trying to solve it, you have daily, direct access to our prime suspect pool. It only makes sense that we take advantage of that."

I couldn't fault them. I'd be doing the same thing if the roles were reversed. I took a bite of pie.

"Are we good?" she asked.

"Yes. Let Nichols know that I'm not trying to cut out the police or trying to solve this case on my own. However, like you said, I'm kind of stuck in the middle of it. I even have some of the guys coming up to me and volunteering information that implicates others in the group."

"Like what?"

"I believe their intent was that it got to you all, but I guess it's simpler for them to tell me. For example, Eric Gamble and Bob Bishop had a real estate business relationship with Doug that went south. Both Eric and Bob believe Doug cheated them out of tens of thousands of dollars, maybe more. You should have Nichols talk to both of them. The three almost came to blows last year. I wasn't here last year, so I can't verify that."

She wrote the names into a small notepad. "Anything else?"

"Just a comment that Doug might have been having an affair down in South America."

"What?"

"Nothing that made sense to me. It's what Bob told me to point me in a different direction away from him. I'll follow up tomorrow, but these guys have really started pointing fingers at each other. If Nichols interviews Eric and Bob, he ought to get more than what they told me."

"Okay."

"Have you all developed anything?" I asked.

"Not really. Lab results are still out. The stuff on you on the internet and from a couple of law enforcement sites was the big news."

"Just trash," I said.

"What time will your group be heading out tomorrow?"

"By seven thirty, why?" I thought I already knew.

"We may want to grab Bob and Eric before they head out."

"That won't make them happy."

"Well, it is a murder investigation."

"I know, just saying. I doubt if they had anything to do with it. It's been over a year, but I guess seeing him again could've set one of them off."

"Think someone else in the group with his own motive may have waited, knowing those two would be the main suspects?"

"That's a good possibility. I'll try to find out more about this affair stuff tomorrow."

"Think they'll get mad at you for prying?" she asked.

"So far, I haven't done any prying. They've come to me and done the talking. I told them early on that the police would handle this, and that there wasn't much I could do."

"Well, they know it became personal when someone tried to kill you. I imagine they expect you to be a little more aggressive now."

"That may have been his biggest mistake. As we've discussed, it narrowed the suspect pool down to someone in the group."

"And how would you narrow it down anymore?"

"Like I said, I'd take out the two tallest and the shortest. I'd take out Tom, and I can't see Dick doing it."

"Dick?"

"Dick Leyes. He's almost as tall as the other two I mentioned, but more significantly, he strikes me as a straight guy. It would have to be something very big to excite him enough to murder."

"Everybody thought Bundy was a great guy, too."

I nodded and ate some more pie. The coffee wasn't very hot, and as though Phil already knew this, he showed up at the table with a fresh pot.

"Let me warm that up a little." He topped off our cups.

"Thanks, Phil. How much does Whip owe you?" Louise asked.

"Oh, don't worry about that. I don't mind treating the police."

"I know, but he takes advantage of that. Take this, I'll get it back from him." She laid a twenty on the table.

"No, no, no, Louise, you don't have to do that," Phil said.

"Take it or throw it in the trash when we leave. It's not like I have anyone else but you to spend it on."

That made Phil smile. "How about your handsome friend here?"

"Don't press your luck," she said. Phil laughed and walked away, leaving the twenty on the table.

"Handsome friend, at least he noticed."

She grinned and said, "His eyesight has been going downhill for a while now."

"Have you talked to Whip about it?"

"Yes, but he's full of himself and the cop image. The fact that Phil has to make a living, too, hasn't made it through Whip's thick skull. He thinks free coffee, donuts, whatever are part of the perks. Other than that and the tough guy image he tries to portray, he's not a bad guy."

"Not one of the ones you were grumbling about earlier?"

"What? Oh, forget that. It's just something that I have to live with. Most guys have matured with the times, but a few are still throwbacks. One in particular always makes comments that could be construed as sexual harassment. Like this afternoon, he says to me that the only reason they picked me to stay close to you was that they knew I had the best chance to suck, with the emphasis on suck, every last drop of information out of you."

"You should at least talk to your chief."

"It's stupid-ass, immature comments. He thinks he's being funny, plus there is always one or two guys that laugh at his remarks and that only encourages him."

"Hopefully, that type of behavior is slowly fading away," I said.

"I doubt if it will ever be gone, but I know it is getting better. I've talked to a few of the older gals, and apparently it was a lot worse back in their day."

"I'm sure it was, but there's still no excuse."

"You know, I was thinking earlier that if you get too close, or if the killer thinks you're getting close to discovering him, he may come after you again. There is a degree of risk in this for you."

"I know."

Chapter 14

When I got back to the hotel room, I stood out on the balcony for a few minutes before getting ready for bed. The moon's reflection created a long path across the ocean's surface toward me. The bright moon even lit up the few low clouds in the sky. A beautiful night, I thought, although standing on the balcony exposed me to an evening sea breeze that seemed unusually cool for this time of the year.

My thoughts surprised me, going back to my ex rather than Rose, my current partner. The divorce had devastated me. I never saw it coming. Too engrossed in my work, I can see now how I took my ex-wife for granted and paid her too little attention. Back then, though, her departure shocked me, and her determination to end our marriage even more so. I thought I had gotten over her, but it was her I suddenly wished could be with me on the balcony.

"Get me a referral?" Tom shouted from his room, interrupting my thoughts.

"Working on it."

He didn't say anything else, and I proceeded to my room in the two-bedroom suite. My head had started hurting, and I wanted to go to sleep.

The inevitable happened on the first tee the next morning. Most knew by the time we gathered at the tee box, but with all thirteen of us bunched together, the rest learned that Bob and Eric had been taken to the police station and wouldn't be playing with us today. All eyes turned toward me with what I hoped was a search for answers and not to steer the blame for all this happening to them.

"What's going on?" Bill Sanchez asked. "Bob was supposed to be in my foursome."

"I believe the police took them both in for questioning," I said.

"Why?" Bill asked, his voice getting sharper.

"Probably because of their issue with Doug. You know they thought he cheated them out of their money," Tom said, coming to my rescue.

"Who told them?"

"Any one of us, Bill," Tom said. "We all witnessed the blowup last year. That is everyone but Jim. He wasn't here."

"Come on, we all know of the animosity between them. How the police learned about it is irrelevant. All of us should have mentioned it to the police when we were questioned," Dick Leyes said.

"Dick's right, so let's just get on with our golf today," Frank said.

Luckily, I didn't have Bill in my foursome, and while James Streelman didn't want to look me in the eye, Ed White and Mike Powers, my cart mate, appeared to be their regular selves. I wondered about Streelman. Was he mad at me, or was he hiding something?

Golf has several beneficial attributes. Despite claims to the contrary, one does get a fair dose of exercise playing eighteen holes. For golfers like us, riding in a cart doesn't take away much of the walking. We spend a lot of our time walking around the rough looking for golf balls. Most of us even like to help others find their golf balls and for a few good reasons. One, and I believe most important, we may find a new golf ball lost by someone else that we can keep; two, we might find our partner's ball for him thus speeding up play; and three, we can keep an eye on him or her to make sure a bad lie doesn't magically turn into a good one.

Golf also helps to take one's mind off the stresses of life, and for four hours, it refocuses that stress, anger, and frustration onto the game of golf. It teaches you that some of the simplest things can become obscenely difficult, like keeping your head down through the swing. There must be some life lesson there that perhaps the wisest have figured out.

Finally, golf gets you out of your house and into the fresh air. Usually this is done with others, so the added benefit of sharing your complaints about politicians, the economy, your spouse, or whatever is possible. I have found that most take advantage of this opportunity.

My game took a slide that day, but the others in my foursome also had a tough day. No one brought up Doug's murder while we were out on the course. We directed most of our comments at the evil streak the course designer had when he laid out the course.

In the club house, however, the topic of the murder resurfaced with the presence of Bob and Eric. Both reported on their experiences with the police without hesitation.

"It wasn't that bad," Eric said in response to Streelman's question. "They tried to interrogate me, but I told them if they kept things civil, I'd answer every question they had. They did, and I did. I had Detective Young. I had to explain the real estate stuff twice to him. I don't think he's that smart. Anyways, once I went through everything and told him I'd welcome his scrutiny of the company's paperwork, he seemed to be satisfied."

"Did he ask you if you killed him?" Jim asked.

"Of course. I told him I would've broken both his knees. I wouldn't have killed him, because I still hoped to get my money back."

Bob stood a few feet away talking to Mike Powers. A few others stood behind Powers, listening but not joining the conversation.

"Nichols was a bit of an ass. He kept acting like he didn't believe me, but I kept my cool. I've watched enough TV to know better. I explained to him that murdering Doug would be illogical. Pulled my Spock card. I think it flustered him, but since I didn't kill Doug, I don't care."

I walked away from the gaggle and bought a pulled pork sandwich for my lunch. A step up from the hot dogs I had for my two prior lunches. Finding an empty seat at Tom's table, I joined Tom and Frank. Frank had finished most of his large chili dog, and seeing it, I immediately second guessed my choice for lunch. Tom had finished his lunch and had not left enough evidence for me to deduce what he had.

"It appears that Bob and Eric didn't suffer too much at the hands of the police today," Tom said.

"And they get to be the center of attention for a while," Frank said.

"Eric told me something interesting. He'll probably tell you, too," Tom said to me.

"What?"

"Eric said that Detective Young gave him his card and said to call him if he could think of anything that might be important. More interesting, he also told Eric that if he couldn't get in touch with him, he could always just pass the information on to you."

"Me?"

"I guess it's because Detective Young knows about your dates with Officer Strong."

"Come on, Tom, you know those aren't dates."

"And whose fault is that? Not hers, she bought you late night pie for two nights in a row."

"Are you dating the blond cop?" Frank asked, obviously happy to get into the pick-on-Jim conversation.

"I've asked Jim to set me up with a friend. She probably has more than one friend, Frank."

"Jim, have you got any selfies with her? Hot tub selfies go viral pretty quick," Frank said.

They both started laughing at their own jokes.

"She gave me a ride back to the hotel after the hospital, and we stopped at a diner. Then last night she asked me to me to meet her there again. It's all case related, and it's nothing I initiated. And, Tom, she wore her uniform both times."

"Just means she's playing hard to get," Tom said.

"I have a feeling, I'm not going to be welcome in this group much longer," I said.

"Don't worry about that. Everyone expects you to be working this with the police. Why do you think Eric approached you in the first place?" Tom said.

"Plus, Tom and I will still like you," Frank laughed at his own comment.

Pete approached us. The sweat stain around the Borden's cap had grown a half an inch.

"I need to sit down. Got too much sun today," he said.

"Are you okay? You look a little flushed. Let me get you some water." Frank hurried over to where a pitcher of water and several glasses sat at the end of the counter.

"I'll be fine," Pete said to us and removed his hat. "Why do most of these cart gals look as old as me? Back home I think there's a rule that you have to be under twenty-five."

"I don't think they can make that a rule," Tom said.

"Should be able to," Pete said. He accepted the glass of water from Frank. "Thanks."

"How'd you shoot today?" Frank asked me.

"Not too good, but I did manage to keep my score under a hundred. How about you?"

"The same. Beautiful course but could do with wider fairways and less water."

Frank's comment caused us all to grin. We were all looking forward to finding the course where the ball always landed in the fairway, and with greens that would always roll the ball to the hole.

As we were loading the car to head back to the hotel, I received a text from Eric. "When we get back, I need to talk to you. Starbucks at two-thirty? Don't tell anyone."

"Okay, see you there." I sent in a return text.

"Problems?" Tom asked.

"Eric wants to talk to me again. Wants to meet me at Starbucks at two thirty. Told me not to tell anyone, so keep it between us."

"Will do. Wonder what he wants."

On the ride back to the hotel, I wondered if I shouldn't have told Tom. What if Eric's information was about Tom? I told him about the text because I was determined not to be pulled in circles by someone else's melodramatics or wild theories. Eric had just come from the police. I hoped he hadn't held something back that he now wanted me to know on the Q. T. That would irritate me.

Chapter 15

Eric stood at the counter, waiting for me to arrive before ordering. He seemed anxious about something.

"What do you want?"

"Grande cappuccino," I said. I didn't need anything, but since this was his meeting, I decided to let him play the good host.

He ordered the same for himself.

"What's up?" I asked while we walked to a nearby table.

"Bob and I want you to talk to Streelman. Bob said he mentioned to you about Doug having an affair."

"Something that happened down in Brazil, right?"

"Yes. Rumor has it that it is not uncommon for the AirExpress guys to carry on a relationship there. The place is overflowing with available women that could use a little extra money. The women even have a network to hook up their friends with interested AirExpress crews. A single school teacher, sales clerk, especially if they have children, need the extra cash and the AirExpress guys have it."

"Why in the world would someone, other than his wife, want to kill Doug over an affair?"

"I don't know," Eric said, "but there might be more to it. Streelman flies to South America, too. He may know something."

"Did you mention it to the police?"

"I didn't think of it. They were focused on me."

"Is Streelman also the guy who Doug allegedly swapped wives with?"

"What? Where'd you hear that? Oh, you're thinking of Vince and his wife and Doug and his wife. Ha! Streelman's wife isn't one that anyone would want to trade for."

"Kind of harsh," I said, but Eric was still grinning.

"You've got to see her. Nice woman, may be a good cook, but no thanks."

"Can you think of anything in Doug's past relationship with Vince or his wife that might have caused Vince to attack Doug?"

"No, besides Vince was the winner in that relationship. Doug's wife is a knockout. Plus, none of us really know if anything ever happened between the four. It's all just gossip. If they were into swapping, none of us ever really knew anything."

"So, no one ever admitted to it."

"No, but they would joke about it and lead us all on."

"They still seemed to be friends," I said.

"Yes, I think they are. Never had a real falling out, as far as I know. It's just the geographic separation kind of killed the tight relationship."

I understood that. My wife and I had close friends at all our assignments, but after moving to a new assignment in some other state or country, the friendship remained but the relationship slowly eroded.

"I have a hard time thinking anyone in our group is guilty of all this, but it almost has to be one of us," I said.

"Why?"

"I was lured to the parking garage by someone claiming to be Detective Nichols. That person knew me, knew Nichols was interviewing us, and knew where my car was parked. That person had to be one of us. That was his big mistake. Before that it could have been anyone. Could have been a nut without even a real motive. After the attack on me, though, the list of suspects shrank to fourteen."

"That's a good point. The guy went after you to stop you from investigating Doug's murder."

"Which was a mistake, because I was doing my best to stay out of the investigation. Now I'm right in the middle of it."

"Well, it wasn't me so you're down to thirteen, and I can't see Bob doing it, so that's twelve. Can you exclude Tom?" Eric asked.

"I think so."

"Well, that brings it down to eleven."

"You hang around with Pete, Frank, and Mike. Can you exclude them?"

"They're on my list of highly unlikely, but I can't exclude them yet. What do you think of Dick?" I figured what the hell, as long as he wanted to talk about people, I might as well let him.

"Leyes, no way. The guy wouldn't cheat in solitaire. Can't see him doing any killing. Now, Edward, Bill, Larry, and both Jims have tempers. I've seen them explode. Back in the days when everyone could drink until they could barely walk in the O'Clubs, tempers would flare, and while I don't know any specifics, I wouldn't be surprised if every one of them got into fights."

Times had changed. When I was a young officer in the air force, heavy drinking was viewed by many as expected. Especially on Friday nights at the Officer Clubs, or O'Clubs as Eric referred to them. Squadron and unit functions frequently turned into wild parties. By the time I retired, however, we referred to that period as the good old days. They weren't, of course.

"The trouble is I don't see a premeditated attack like the one on Doug or myself as an anger issue. Although it's possible someone could let it simmer for a long time. By the way, you said both Jim's. You mean James and Jim?" I asked.

"Yes, you can call Streelman either, but with Jim M here, we usually call Streelman James, since that is what he goes by anyway. Plus, with you here, it would get really confusing. I don't know, this whole this is strange. I should go. Don't tell anyone I've been talking to you. We good, Jim?"

"Yes, Eric, we're good."

He got up and hurried out of Starbucks. I sat there, thinking about the situation and wishing I hadn't come on this trip.

"How'd that happen?" the young barista asked. She had walked up behind me.

"This?" I asked. A stupid response, of course, as I saw her staring at my bandage when I turned around. She had been in the Starbucks every time I had. She was short and slender with jet black hair accentuated with a few dark blue streaks. I didn't think she was out of her teen years yet.

"Yes. You were the guy attacked in the garage, right?"

"That's me."

"It was one of the guys in your group who was killed, too. I saw the news. Scary. That happened right here."

By right here, I knew she meant the adjacent parking garage, referring to the attack on me, not the murder.

"You don't happen to know who did it?"

"No. No one does. Are you going to be okay? You have a black eye."

"Luckily it didn't crack my skull."

"Good thing it didn't hit your eye either."

"That's true. I should have a nice scar, though. Might make me look handsome."

"Distinguished, that's the look you want. Old men don't look handsome." She blushed and her hand went to her mouth. "I didn't mean that the way it sounded."

"I'll settle for distinguished."

She turned around and returned to her spot behind the counter. I headed back to the hotel room.

"How'd it go? I saw Eric leave," Tom said.

"Went fine, but I didn't learn anything new."

"To be expected."

"Hey, you think you and I are still handsome?"

"Of course. Why?"

"Just something somebody said."

Chapter 16

Pete pulled me aside before the five thirty meeting started. We went out into the hall to talk.

"Has anyone mentioned the trouble between Bill Sanchez and Doug that happened a while back when we were all in the air force?"

"No, I don't think so. What happened?"

"Doug turned him in for drinking heavily the night before he was scheduled to fly."

"Can't do that?"

"You have a time window. In this case, Bill had been drinking into the wee hours and had an early morning flight."

"Is that common?"

"No to both. Not common for a pilot to do that and not common for someone to turn him in if he did. Probably the right thing for Doug to have done, but it messed over Bill. I had forgotten about it."

"Does Bill still carry a grudge?"

"Not to my knowledge, I think he knew he had no one to blame but himself. Yet, it messed with his career, so it may be festering deep down. Something else may have happened more recently that set him off. I don't know, but I just wanted to let you know."

"Okay," I said.

"They're not going to catch him, are they?"

"We'll see. There's not much time left, but who knows? Do

you know if there was anything to this wife swapping story?"

"You mean with Vince and his wife?"

"Yes."

"Could be something there, but I've never heard anything in it that would tell me any bad blood came out of it. They seemed to still be good friends. Still married to the same wives, too." He looked at his watch, "Guess we should get to the meeting."

At the meeting I learned my shot on the par three seventh hole had won closest to the hole. I gladly took my winnings of twenty-five dollars, even though the shot hadn't been a great one. I scalded a six iron, and the ball bounced and rolled all the way to the green.

Everyone throws in fifty dollars at the beginning of the week and, if we're lucky, we win our money back before going home. There are other prizes, but with my golf game, I don't get too excited.

After the meeting, I walked with my same dinner gang to a nearby pub for beer and hamburgers. Before we got there, I received a text from Louise. She wanted me to meet her again but said no pie tonight. She had something else planned for us.

"Your lady friend?" Tom asked.

"Yes." I kept her text to myself. If I said she had something else planned for us, I would never hear the end of it during dinner. I imagined everyone would jump on the chance to give me a hard time.

"You know," LG said during dinner, "the police told both Bob and Eric that they should tell you if they think of anything and can't reach them. I think they are setting you up for another attack."

I had already considered that. "Maybe, but since someone

already tried to take me out, I think the consensus is he won't try again."

"This guy isn't being rational," Mike said. "Who knows what he'll do."

"True, but I don't plan on making it easy for him. You know, fool me once, shame on you, fool me twice, shame on me. I give him guts, though, for staying after he attacked me. He took a big gamble. I could've recognized him."

"Still, for the next three days, we'll be keeping our eyes on you, and we'll be sure to let everyone else know what we are doing, so that should also discourage him," LG said.

"I appreciate it, but, like I said, I doubt if he'll try anything more. You guys are making me feel like I should be buying your dinner tonight."

"Better tonight than at the steakhouse on Thursday night," Pete said.

"Especially since we all got the happy hour special," Tom said.

Despite a couple of their half-hearted protests, I did pick up the bill that night. After dinner, Tom offered to ride along with me to meet with Louise.

"Tomorrow," I said. "Let me give her a heads-up first."

"Okay, but you're not making this bodyguard business easy."

"Thanks. I do appreciate it."

The garage was dark when I walked over to get my car, and I'd be lying if I didn't admit that every noise had me looking around. Ten minutes later, halfway to the diner, a jacked-up, dark Toyota Tundra raced up behind my Mustang. It followed barely a foot behind my car with its headlights on high, glaring through my back window for about ten seconds. Suddenly, without signaling, it shot around me, passing with a loud roar of its engine.

I never saw the driver and fought the urge to speed up after the idiot. By the time I reached the diner my blood pressure had returned to normal.

"Hey," I said to Louise as I closed the door to the Mustang.

"Thought we'd do something different tonight. I assume you've already eaten." She wore jeans and a light pink blouse.

"Almost didn't recognize you out of uniform. You look nice," I said. "Not that you didn't before. I didn't mean that."

She grinned. "I got off early today. Had to see the dentist, so I thought we could go somewhere else, if that's okay with you."

"Fine by me."

"I'll drive us. It's not far, but it's a little tricky to get there." She pointed to a small silver Honda parked a few spaces away, and we got in.

"Hope the dentist didn't pull out too many teeth."

"Don't joke. He said he needs to take out my wisdom teeth. I guess they should've been removed years ago. How'd your day go?"

"Good, I won closest to the hole but then spent all my winnings buying dinner for some of the guys."

"Win a lot?"

"No, not enough to pay for dinner."

"Nichols doesn't think the business angle between Bishop, Gamble and our victim is much of a motive. Too long ago, and we couldn't find any reference to it in any of his social media, emails, or messages from his phone or laptop. The thinking is there would've been some sort of a threat in there at some point in the last three or four months."

"I don't think it is either."

She pulled onto a narrow side road and then turned behind a bank building onto a well driven dirt road for about fifty yards, before turning into a dirt parking lot surrounded by trees. Next to the lot, stood what looked like an old wooden building not much bigger than a house.

"This is Willard's, my favorite place to drink Cosmopolitans. For obvious reasons, I don't like coming alone, so thanks for letting me drag you here."

The parking lot had one pole light that lit up the seven or eight cars parked in the lot.

"It is a little spooky out here."

"I'll protect you," she laughed.

We walked in through a side door. The place smelled of smoke and fried seafood. All four tables were occupied, and everyone looked up at us when we walked in.

"Spooky in here, too," I said.

"We're going out front." She led me out the front door to a large wooden deck and to the one vacant table out of five that were spread across the deck.

"Now this is nice," I said. "I like the view, especially with the moon tonight."

"I like the sound of the waves."

The Atlantic Ocean was a mere thirty yards away.

"I'm surprised the owner hasn't expanded the deck or the insides. This is a choice location despite the dirt road."

"The owner likes it just the way it is. Hasn't changed a thing since I started coming here about seven years ago. Mostly employs family and a few old acquaintances."

A server brought her a large cosmopolitan and asked me what

I would like to order. He looked like he was my age and wore the thickest glasses I had seen on someone in a long time. I asked for a Yuengling on tap.

"Thanks, Steve," Louise said as he went to fetch my beer. "Another reason I like this place. They remember you and what you like."

"You must be a regular."

She grinned. "Did you see me nod at him when we came in?"

"No."

"That's how he knew I wanted my usual. Can you believe the state boys have already backed out of the investigation?"

"They always limit their help to two days?"

"No, but as the saying goes, most murders are solved in the first forty-eight hours, or they're never solved. In these higher profile cases they like to show up at the beginning. That way if it's solved, they can take some of the credit. Once they decide it will likely not be solved, they're happy to back away and go home."

"Their stats probably look good," I said.

"Right. Anything new coming out of the group?"

"I'm not sure you can do anything with it, but Doug apparently turned Sanchez in for drinking before a flight many years ago that may have messed up Sanchez' air force career. I don't see anything there unless something else happened since."

She made a note on a small paper pad. "We identified the foursome Doug hit his ball into on the golf course. They were all at their hotel bar during the time the murder took place."

"I couldn't see them killing someone for that. Happens all the time, and the ball didn't hit a person. Did you all talk to LG or Streelman about that story of the AirExpress guys having affairs in Brazil?"

"No one thinks that would be very significant. In fact, Detective Young said that sort of behavior should be expected."

"Maybe, but it's sad to think we should expect that behavior."

The server brought my beer to the table. "Thanks. I get the tab, not her," I said. She didn't argue.

"Doug got a phone call from Edward White an hour before he was killed. Do you have any idea what that was about? Has he mentioned anything about talking to him that afternoon?"

"No, not that I heard. Are you all going to ask him?"

"I think Nichols is doing that right now. He's also going to talk to Doug's roommate again. The feeling is that he should have known where Doug was. In the first go around though, he denied it."

"It does make sense he would have mentioned what he was doing when he left the room, but maybe he wasn't there at the time," I said.

"Probably be what he'll claim. He was supposed to be at dinner with you that night. The five of you often dined together?"

"That was only our second night, and we all ate together the first night. It's their tradition. I was included the night of the incident primarily because I'm sharing a hotel suite with Tom."

"How did they each react to that initial phone call?"

"I felt like the news of Doug's death hit all of them pretty hard. I've tried to think back if any one of them took the news different, but they all had that shocked and confused look. Additionally, nothing has been mentioned since that has indicated that any of the four have had any past issues with Doug."

"You think it's safe to narrow our list down to exclude them?"

"With the time left, I would. I mean who knows, but my money is that it's one of the other ten."

"Except the tallest and shortest?"

"That's right. Makes your list even smaller."

"It's still a long list with so little to work with," she said.

"Yes," but I wondered which of them had been worried enough about my presence to try to kill me?

Chapter 17

Tom remained quieter than usual on the drive next morning to Bear Hollow. I hadn't played the course before, but the guys referred to it as a swamp. It didn't sound like one of their favorite courses.

"Why did you all pick Bear Hollow? It didn't sound like anyone was too enthusiastic about playing it today."

"It comes with the package. If we want to play some of the more expensive courses then we have to also play some of the cheaper places. Despite their whining about the course, most of us like the wildlife that's on the course."

"You mean the alligators?"

Tom smiled. "Yes, but there is a large lake on the course that is home to thousands of turtles and birds. Snakes, too. They have a handout in the clubhouse discussing the various animals that call Bear Hollow their home."

"Any bears?"

"Interestingly, no, but they have the most aggressive squirrels there. They'll get in your golf cart as soon as you get out to scavenge for any loose food."

"We had some of those yesterday," I said.

"I brought my insecticide. Let me spray your legs and arms when we get there. They have a lot of small, nasty black or blue flies that bite."

"Are you kidding me? Sounds like we're going into the jungle."

"Next best thing," he said.

"By the way, Louise said she'd be happy for you to join us tonight."

He grinned and turned the car into the clubhouse parking lot.

The golf course didn't turn out like anything I had imagined. I thought it looked nice with well-manicured fairways and greens. The rough turned into thick undergrowth a few yards off the fairway, and I lost two balls during the front nine. Still, I shot a forty-two and thought I had a good chance to shoot in the mid-eighties by the time I finished.

On the eleventh hole I shanked my drive into the heavy underbrush on the right. Dick Leyes drove the cart I rode in and had been having a fairly good day himself. Unfortunately, on this hole, he pulled his drive into the rough on the left. He dropped me off to look for my ball and went off to search for his own.

Streelman and Sanchez were in the other cart and came over like they were going to help me search for my ball. Instead, they pulled up close.

"See that path that cuts through to the other fairway. I think it kicked hard right and went down toward the old bridge that takes you across. Take a look down there, but watch out for critters," Sanchez said, and they both laughed.

Streelman steered their cart back into the fairway and toward their golf balls.

I didn't see my ball bounce anywhere in the rough, but it seemed like their advice was as good as anything I had planned to find my ball. I had to walk about ten yards farther in direction of the green before I saw the path. Wide enough for utility equipment or maybe a golf cart, it clearly wasn't maintained as weeds and grasses had grown into the sides.

Once on the path, I could see the bridge and walked slowly toward it, looking on both sides of the path for my ball. The area turned out to be a good, golf ball hunting ground. I found three fairly nice golf balls in the process but not mine. I was wondering why people abandoned their golf balls so easily here when a loud crunching of leaves and twigs followed by a large alligator rushing out of the underbrush toward me.

I reacted by taking four or five quick steps backwards. In my panic, I almost fell over which would have been disastrous. The alligator stopped and glared at me. I turned and ran back to the fairway. When I reached the fairway and looked back, the alligator was gone. I stood there, breathing heavily but maintaining my watch on the path.

"Jim, Jim, are you alright? What did you see?" Dick said from the cart as he pulled alongside.

"An alligator. A big one charged me."

"But are you okay?"

"Yes. I think I'll take the penalty."

My blood pressure didn't get below a thousand until we finished the hole. The double bogey I made felt almost a relief after surviving the alligator attack. The next hole happened to be the one that paralleled the one we just played and brought us down past the bridge. From this fairway, we had an unobstructed view of the bridge. The creek under it bent and cut across the fairway.

"Oh yeah, I remember," Dick said.

"What?"

"This is where an old female alligator has her nest. You should never have gone in there. If I had remembered, I would have warned you."

"Sanchez told me he saw my ball bounce down the path toward the bridge."

"What? And neither he nor Streelman warned you?"

"They did say watch out for the critters or something like that."

Dick looked around until he saw the two in their cart about twenty yards behind us. Both were looking at us and smiling.

"Let it be," I said.

Dick looked away from the two and shook his head. "This is no good. I may not come back next year. They could've got you killed, and now they're grinning like it was a big joke."

"No joke to me. It almost had me for lunch."

"Bastards," Dick said.

Later, on the green, Streelman came up to me. "Did you see the gator? You came out of there like it was about to chase you down."

"Not funny. It charged at me. If I slipped, it would have gotten me."

"A million people a day play this course, and no one has ever been hurt by a gator. Get over it." He walked away from me.

I wondered if to them it truly was just a big joke, or if one of them would like to have me no longer around. Both individuals had to know they were near the top of the not-so-short list of suspects.

Nothing else happened on the course, and both Dick and I managed to shoot matching eighty-nines. We felt some satisfaction in the fact that we beat both Bill and James, who shot ninety-one and ninety-three. Still, once back in the clubhouse, Dick made a bee line to the two and proceeded to let them know their joke was a bad one.

I wanted to tell Dick to forget it but decided not to get involved. I walked out of the snack bar and into the golf shop. On the wall were two framed newspaper articles about golfers getting killed by alligators on the course some twelve years earlier. The "killer gator" was captured and "humanely put down."

Next to the cashier, a short pile of fliers sat next to a sign that said take one. Picking one up, I saw a map of the course and three areas where golfers were cautioned not to go on foot. One was by the old bridge where Sanchez and Streelman told me to look for my golf ball.

During the drive back to the hotel, Tom asked, "Did Bill and James really send you in the area near the bridge to look for your ball?"

"Yes. They thought it was funny."

"You see the gator?"

"Almost too late. It charged me, and I almost fell trying to get away."

"Damn, that's not good. I can't believe they would do that."

"They thought it was just a big joke."

"I've never seen it there, but a number of the guys saw it sunning itself next to the bridge last time we were here. They said it was a big one."

"It looked huge to me. I felt lucky to get away and amazed I didn't ruin my underwear."

Tom grinned, "I wouldn't be able to joke about it."

"I didn't think it was very funny at the time. Now I just wonder if it was their way of getting me off the investigation."

"You think one of those two killed Doug?"

"I have no idea, but they had to have a reason to send me in there. Like you said, it wasn't a very good joke."

"No, it wasn't."

I wondered if I should tell Louise about the incident. On the one hand, they should never have recommended I go looking for the golf ball near the bridge. On the other, I felt like it was somewhat childish to run to Louise, saying the two picked on me. Nothing came of it, but they should never have done it. I'd give it some thought, but either way, I had a nasty feeling about the whole matter.

By the time we arrived back at the hotel, I had forced the issue to the back of my mind.

Chapter 18

The five thirty meeting started at five o'clock again, because six of the local golf courses had gotten together and were hosting a happy hour behind the hotel. Everyone was in a hurry to get to the happy hour, so the meeting only lasted twenty minutes. It was our night to have the meeting in our room. After the meeting, Tom and I lingered a while after everyone left in order to rearrange the furniture in the room.

"I'm surprised my run in with the gator didn't come up during the meeting despite most everyone knowing about it by now."

"I wondered about that, too, but I think it might have been a touchy subject. The guys didn't want it to spiral into a divisive shouting match. There are a few guys very upset about what Bill and James did."

"And some others who thought it was just a joke, no big deal," I said.

"Surprisingly so. I received a few texts about it before the meeting. Let's head down before the free beer disappears. Probably half the people in this hotel are golfers."

As we walked down the short hallway, I glanced into my room and saw a folded sheet of paper on my bedroom floor.

"Hold on," I said. Tom opened the door to go outside but stopped.

I picked up the paper, a plain white sheet of bond paper. Unfolding it, I saw a handwritten note saying, "You may want to leave now. Tomorrow the alligator may be faster."

I handed it to Tom. He read it. "Damn, this is just getting worse." He handed it back to me. "Are you going to show this to Louise?"

"I guess we shouldn't have touched it, but this could be from anyone. Doesn't prove anything. Still, I'll give it to her," I said and folded the paper, sticking it in a back pocket.

"You probably wish you didn't come this year," Tom said.

"An understatement," I said.

"Sorry, man. First, you get bashed in the head and then attacked by an alligator. Have you been telling Rose all about this?"

Tom knew about Rose, my partner, as we had discussed her a couple times. "No, she would tell me to go home, too. I don't want to leave until the week is over. If I left early, it would feel like I was running away. Besides, I don't like being pushed around."

It seemed like the entire hotel had emptied and come to the happy hour. The line for the free beer had at least thirty people in it. Still, it was free, and the bartenders were pouring beer into the cups from pitchers as fast as they could, so Tom and I got in line.

I saw Streelman, Sanchez, and Larry Brown at a table. They looked at us but didn't smile. Tom noticed them, too.

"It's like you did something to them, rather than the other way around," he said.

"I think they're worried now about me telling the police what they did."

"You should."

"Not tonight, I just got a text from Louise cancelling our date."

"It's a date now," Tom's face lit up. "Way to go."

Edward White and Vince Flores joined the other three. "I think what you have there is that part of our group who thought sending you into the briar patch was a good joke," Tom said.

I didn't have the heart to tell Tom that the briar patch worked the other way around, but I knew what he meant.

We finally got our beer and a free hot dog and headed over to join a number of the guys crowded around a table. Pete stood next to the table and was explaining something to three women.

"Oh, God, I can tell you right now what Pete is saying." The three women feigned laughing and walked away.

"What's that?"

"He's wearing his Young Academy tee shirt. You can special order those from some novelty shops. He loves to explain to anyone that the Young Academy is a very progressive institute of higher learning where all bad girls get a free ride."

"I take it there is no real Young Academy," I said.

"Right on. His pitch is that he's the professor, and he's always on the search for bad girls."

"He's single, right?"

"Yes. Been married twice. I think his jokes drove them both away." Tom shook his head. "But we love him."

As if he heard us, Pete walked around the table to greet us.

"Hey guys, you just missed them."

"The three women?" Tom asked.

"Yes, they're part of that group of women that come down from Canada every year."

"I thought so," Tom said.

The three of us moved to the short concrete wall that served as the boundary of the patio. We sat on it and spent the next thirty minutes watching the crowd and discussing what we thought about a few professional golfers.

I felt my phone buzz in my pocket and saw that it was a short text from Louise. "Can you please come to 1824 Myrtle St. It's important and will only take a minute. Can't talk right now."

I glanced up and saw Tom watching me. "Are we back on?"

"No, she just wants me to come see her. Said it would only take a minute."

"Oh, so she has had sex with you," Tom said.

Pete laughed.

"No, no such luck. Said she can't talk right now. I should be back before this thing breaks up," I said.

"Doubt that. They just ran out of free beer," Tom said.

"You going to see that blond cop?" Pete said.

"Yes." I stood up.

"Want us to ride along?"

"No thanks, Pete, she said it would just be for a minute." I could see Tom wanted to repeat his joke, so I didn't look back as I left.

I put the address in my phone, and using a navigation app, I reached the location in ten minutes. The small, blue house sat in the middle of the block with several other similar houses on both sides of the street. I parked on the street and saw an older couple walking a very small dog away from me on the sidewalk across the street. Otherwise, the street showed no signs of life.

A light shown through the front window of the house. The blinds were open, but I didn't see anyone inside. I wondered if this was Louise' house and called her phone number. After getting no answer, I approached the front door. A small crack of light filled a space where the door was ajar. The small hairs on the back of my neck began dancing as I sensed something was not right.

A quick debate in my mind resulted with me calling out to her. Announcing myself to someone waiting to spring a trap on me or an intruder could be foolish, but getting shot by Louise, thinking I was someone breaking in wouldn't be too smart either.

"Louise! Louise, it's me, Jim." I called out loud enough for her to hear me in the back of the house.

No one answered, but I heard a noise like something falling off a desk or table onto the wooden floor. The noise came from the room to my right. I could see the door to the room a few steps in front of me.

"Louise," I said again and walked toward the door.

It's funny how the mind works. In those few steps, my brain ran through hundreds of scenarios with most telling me this wasn't right. If this was a movie, the background music would be building up to the point where the audience would all be thinking "don't go in there." In real life, there is no background music, and my mind kept arguing with itself.

Reaching the doorway, I took a step into the room to look around. I saw a toy car, one of those remote-control-kind, on the floor. I started to call out again when I sensed more than heard someone coming at me from behind. Instinctively, I looked back and my body tensed. A man I didn't recognize swung a wooden, kitchen rolling pin at my head.

"Wait!" I said, not able to get more out before blocking the blow with my left forearm. I wanted to tell him it was a mistake, but he either had no desire to hear me or worse. His left hand streaked for my throat, and I swatted it away with my right. He tried hitting me again with the rolling pin, but I was able to grab it and yank it down and away from him.

Any thoughts I may have had at the moment that once I got the rolling pin away from him that he might calm down were short lived. He snarled and leapt on me. I realized at that point that this was all a setup, and for whatever reason, this man was out to hurt me if not kill me. His eyes displayed anger if not outright hatred. I knew I had to stop trying to figure out why this was happening and focus on keeping myself alive.

The realization that his intent now was to get me into a choke hold further erased any hesitation I had to end this in a peaceful compromise. If I hadn't tossed the rolling pin away, I would've used it on his head. Instead, I twisted and stepped away to give me enough space to hit him on the nose with a left jab. As his head popped backwards, I immediately struck at his throat with the knuckles on my flat right hand bent under. Unfortunately, he moved sideways enough to limit the impact.

Snarling, he leapt at me again. This time he succeeded in knocking me back against the table, and we both fell to the floor. I tried to back away from him, but he crawled after me, grabbing the collar of my shirt. It's hard to fight anyone in a tangled mess, rolling around on the ground or, in our case, the floor. It's extremely tiring, and it's where the fighting can get very dirty.

The first chance I could, I got my leg into position to push myself up and away from him. He didn't want to let go and made the mistake of looking up at me. His face gave me a good opportunity to slam a short right jab into his already bruised nose.

He squealed and jerked his head back. Blood began to flow from his nose, but rather than stop, he growled and charged into me.

By now, though, the surprise of the attack and the confusion in my mind were gone. I finally felt in control, and as his body started to slam against me, I twisted, grabbed him, and used his own momentum to throw him into the wall. He collapsed onto the floor, but immediately struggled to get back up.

"Stay down!" I tried to sound forceful, but I was gasping for air.

"Darren! Stay down, or I will shoot you and feed you to the gators!"

I looked back and saw Officer Louise Strong standing behind me. She looked furious, and I thought for a second she might shoot him. Her right hand was on her weapon, but she had not drawn it.

"Jim, I'm so sorry."

I looked at her and then back at Darren, who had slid back down the wall and was sitting on the floor, his face in his hands.

"What is all this? Why did you text me to come here?"

"I didn't."

That didn't answer any of my questions. I noticed a plain wooden chair in the corner by the window. A coil of rope had been placed on the seat.

"Where's my phone Darren?" she asked.

"On the kitchen counter," he said.

"Would you go get it," she asked me.

I did.

"I'm calling your mom, Darren. Okay?"

"His mom?" I asked, thinking this guy was at least thirty-five.

She raised her hand at me, "Later."

I stepped out into the hallway. I wanted to yell at her, to tell her the guy belongs in jail.

"Darren, you feeling alright?

"No, my nose hurts."

"I'll get you something for it." Rather than moving, she asked me to see if I could find some ice and a washcloth in the kitchen. She did say please, and that one word led me to realize there was a lot more to this than I realized.

While I was going through kitchen drawers looking for a washcloth, I heard her talking to someone on the phone. I could see a reflection of myself in the kitchen window. My face didn't look any worse from the altercation, but the bandage over my eye had partially come loose. I pressed it back down against the skin. A small bowl next to the sink served as something I could put ice in, and I was returning to her when she and Darren walked into the kitchen.

"Sit at the table Darren, and I'll help you get cleaned up. Jim, you might as well sit here, but first, could you get the washcloth wet." I did, resisting a strong desire to walk out of the house. I didn't need any of this, but I was curious. She motioned to the chair opposite Darren. The table was a small square one. She pulled out the chair to Darren's left.

I put the washcloth and the ice in front of her but didn't sit down. She immediately started working on Darren's face.

"Darren, what were you thinking? Jim is not my boyfriend. He's helping me out with a police investigation. Do you understand?"

Darren glanced at me, the rage gone from his face, before he turned his head and continued staring at Louise.

"Is this why you took my phone?" she asked.

"Yes, I saw you with him. I'm sorry Louise, but I went crazy again. I didn't want him to be with you. I wasn't going to hurt him. I was just going to tie him up until he promised me he would leave you alone."

"Then what was the rolling pin for?" I asked, doing my best not to shout the question.

"I was just going to knock you out, so I could tie you to the chair. That's all."

"That would've been bad, Darren. Even though you wouldn't have meant to, you might have hurt Jim."

I wanted to shout out that of course he wanted to hurt me and to ask if they were both crazy. However, the realization that one of them might be held me back, and I didn't need Louise criticizing me for not being politically correct with my terminology. Safer to get my head bashed in these days.

"Jim, please check the pantry for some Fig Newtons."

I did so, and seeing that there were only three left in the package, I considered cramming them in my mouth in front of the jerk. I gave the package to Louise.

"Here you go, Darren. Now isn't there something you should say to Jim?"

"Thank you."

"And," she said.

"I'm sorry. I thought you were trying to be Louise' boyfriend."

"That wouldn't have mattered, Darren. You can't hurt someone just because he might be my boyfriend. That's still not right."

He didn't say anything. His mind appeared to be focused on the cookies. He broke all three cookies into two pieces before he started eating the first one.

Louise looked at me, and I saw that she had a tear trying to escape from her left eye. She dabbed at it with the back of her hand.

"Louise!" a woman called from the front door.

"In the kitchen, Emma."

I could hear Emma talking to someone who must have been with her. A second later, a slim woman with long silver hair walked into the kitchen. She wore a short sleeve blue sweater, a pair of jeans, and pink tennis shoes. She looked at the three of us.

"Is everyone okay?"

Chapter 19

"You've got blood on your shirt," I said.

Louise looked down at her pink tee shirt before closing the front door.

"I'm so sorry, Jim. Come back into the kitchen, I'll make some coffee and try to make some sense of all this for you."

"Is this your place?" I asked, following her to the kitchen. I sat down at the table.

"No, it's Darren's. Well, it's really Emma's, I think. Darren lives here when he's not away."

"Away?"

She looked back at me for a second before pouring the water into the small Keurig coffee maker. She started the brew cycle and turned around, leaning against the counter.

"I grew up next door to Darren. He's had emotional, mental, call it what you want adjustment issues since he was a kid. Because of this, I guess I was his only real friend. At school he was bullied, and his family finally had to send him to a private school that specialized with children like him. I don't think it was much better."

"You're a good person, Louise," I said, getting a picture to where this was going.

"He can be a very nice person. He's not dumb, but sometimes he doesn't correctly process information, and he has a quick temper. Emma is a saint. Her husband couldn't stand dealing with Darren and gave her an ultimatum. Put Darren away forever, or he was going to leave her. She picked Darren and has been dealing with him on her own since he was a teenager."

"Where does he go when he's away?"

"A state facility. One of the good ones, luckily. One of the perks of this job is that I know the good ones from the bad. The first time he got into trouble with the law they put him in a state prison. Luckily, I pushed hard to get him transferred, and the prison doctors saw right away that I was right. He's been in and out since. Mostly out thankfully. I've had many dinners right here with Emma and Darren in the past decade."

"Does Emma live here?"

"No, but she spends most of her time here while Darren is out."

"He's a big guy. I would think you'd need to be very careful with him."

I could see the anger leap into her eyes, but she held back a quick reply. "That's why I started working out."

"How did he know you and I were meeting?"

"He followed me, us, last night and got the wrong idea, obviously. He's only been out a few days. When I got home today, he was waiting for me at my house. We had a coke on the front porch, and we talked about Emma's upcoming birthday. He did make the comment that he saw me last night. That was it, nothing more. I never suspected a thing. However, about an hour ago, I realized my phone was missing, and I remembered Darren went in to use the bathroom before he left."

"So, you thought he might have taken it?"

"I knew he had it. He borrows my things. Always has, but I had no idea that he was going to use it to get you over here."

"I thought it was your house. So now you know how easy I am."

Louise smiled, "True, but scary to think you might fall for something like this again."

Good point, I thought. Twice in one week, what had I said? Fool me twice, shame on me.

She got up, brought me a cup of coffee, and started one for herself.

"You have a key to this place?"

"Yes. Several years back I think Emma decided I was the daughter she never had, and, I guess, we've both always considered me the sister Darren never had. Same grade, same school, next door, it just seemed destined, and poor Darren can be so sweet."

"He's never posed a threat to you?" I asked.

"Not a physical one. He's tried to get amorous on a few occasions. Like I said, that's why I started working out."

I didn't know what to say about that and decided to stay away from the topic.

"Is your arm the only place he hurt you?"

I looked down at my left arm and saw a nasty knot had formed on the side of arm about halfway between my wrist and my elbow.

"Yes. Looks worse than it feels."

"I'm glad nothing worse happened."

"What will happen to him now?"

"The terms of his release are very specific. He can stay out until he does something he shouldn't, like this. He'll go back to the hospital, stay at least a week, be reevaluated and counseled. Emma will visit him a lot. It's important he doesn't feel like he's being abandoned."

"Is he on medication?"

"Some, as little as possible. It's not like the old days."

"I guess there's no chance he was behind my earlier attack?"

"No," Louise said. "Besides, I had only met you then, and Darren was just being released. Afraid not." She stood up to get her coffee.

"You might want to rinse that spot," I said, referring to the blood on her tee shirt. She also wore blue jeans with her police badge exposed on her belt next to her holster.

Before she could comment, her phone rang. She answered it while she grabbed her coffee cup. I could tell from the brief conversation that Emma had called to give her an update.

"The woman who came with Emma, I guess you didn't see her, was his nurse. She's been helping Emma out for the last ten or so years. Darren likes her, too, so that's good. The two of them are taking him straight to the state hospital. It's about an hour from here. He's been given a sedative. They'll treat his nose there, too. You know you broke it."

"I figured. It's not like I didn't try to talk to him to stop him from fighting me in the first place," I said, wondering why I needed to explain anything. "How did he even know to text me?"

"He's not dumb. He knows how to use a phone, and I don't hide your texts. He figured it out." She reached out and put her hand over mine. "Take me back to my house. It's close by."

Chapter 20

"What time did you get in last night?" Tom asked while we walked to breakfast.

"Fine bodyguard you are," I said.

"Any pictures you can share?"

"You know you're sick."

"As they come. What happened to your arm?"

I bent my arm to get a better look at the nasty looking, bluish knot. "Long, very strange story. I'm fine."

"Strange is often good."

"Not that kind, unfortunately."

"Tom, Jim, wait up." I turned and saw Frank Derby jogging up to us. "Did you hear about Bill?"

"What?" we both said.

"He's gone. Drove off about five this morning. No explanation."

"He went home?" Tom asked.

"No one knows. He left a note telling Vince he wouldn't be back."

"Think he could've done it?" Tom asked me.

"I have no idea. It's dumb for him to just leave like this."

"Yeah, I agree," Frank said, and Tom nodded.

"He's not going to be able to hide, and they will go looking for him," I said.

"You better send Louise a text," Tom said.

"I'd rather someone else did."

"You don't cherish your role?"

"No, I don't."

"Doesn't matter, Jim. Everyone else expects you to fill it. Not just us, I think the police do too. Besides, none of us want to contact the police or have them contact us," Frank said.

"A couple of the guys are already complaining about how long it's taking you to solve it," Tom said.

"He's only half joking," Frank said.

We went inside to the buffet line.

"I hate it when the bacon is down to the last few broken pieces in the grease," Frank said, but he still took a half dozen broken pieces.

Two more of the group came over together to tell us of Bill's departure.

"You notice they were really looking at you when they told us," Frank said.

"I know." I took my phone out of my pocket and sent Louise a text. "There, they know."

"Oh, God, not that shirt again," Frank said.

I looked up and saw Pete walking into the restaurant wearing a tan tee shirt with some writing on it that I couldn't make out.

"The guy has issues," Tom said. Despite his remark, he waved Pete to come over. "We've got an open chair, if you want to join us."

"Save it," Pete replied, as he headed for the buffet.

"What does it say?" I asked.

"Something like Young's Counseling Service, specializing in alcoholism, sadomasochism, and sex addiction," Frank said.

"I guess he doesn't embarrass easily."

"No, he doesn't," Tom said.

"Hear about Bill?" Pete asked when he joined us. His plate was piled high with bacon.

"Yes," we all said at the same time.

"They brought out new bacon," Tom said.

"It's going fast, you better get back up there if you want some."

"That line looks too long," Tom said.

As Pete turned to look at the line, Tom grabbed two pieces of bacon off Pete's plate.

"Hey, try that again and I'll stab you with my fork," Pete said, gripping his fork.

The three of us laughed, and even Pete grinned. He still had four or five strips of bacon on his plate.

"I figured out why this game of golf is so hard. I was reading a book on golf the other day and you know there are like forty-three things to remember to do while making each swing of the club. Forty-three. I don't even remember to pull my zipper up on my pants half the time. How can I remember forty-three things?" Pete said.

"Keep your head down, accelerate through the ball, rotate, etc., etc. You're right, there are too many things to remember," Tom said.

"Then you have to remember where you hit your ball," I said.

"Half of these guys can't remember how many times they hit their ball on each hole," Frank said, causing everyone to laugh again.

"Can't always blame them. It's easy to think you only hit your ball six times when you've really hit it seven," Tom said.

Our day out golfing went by without incident. Afterwards, at lunch most of the conversation centered around LG, who almost made a hole in one on the par three fourth hole. Pete received almost as much attention as he made the circuit around the room making sure everyone knew he got the phone number of one of the women driving the refreshment carts around the course.

"It was the shirt. She said she could use some counseling," he said.

A few of the guys responded by saying he was the one that needed counseling, but their comments didn't seem to bother Pete at all.

"He's in his own little world," Tom said to me when we got up to leave.

My phone buzzed while Tom drove us out of the course's parking lot.

"That was Detective Nichols. He wants to meet us at the hotel at two. We should be back by then, right?"

"We should."

"Okay, I'll give him our room number."

"He wants both of us?" Tom asked.

"He didn't specify, but you know everything I do."

Tom didn't respond, but he made a face like he'd rather not be there. "What do you think is up?"

"No telling, probably nothing, although they may have found Bill."

"Would they arrest him?"

"Not technically, but they'll likely drag him back here."

"Will they tell us where they are with the investigation? I would like to hear that. What if this thing goes unsolved?"

"They won't share much, but we might learn a little. If the killer stays quiet and doesn't do anything else stupid, he may well get away with it."

"That would suck," Tom said.

"Yes, it would, but he already made one mistake attacking me, so he may make more. If he does, he'll get caught, but hopefully, no one else will get hurt."

We didn't have to wait long in our hotel room before we heard a knock on the door. I answered it and greeted both Detectives Nichols and Young.

"Ganging up on us today?" I said, half joking while letting them in. Neither seemed to appreciate my comment. "You remember my roommate Tom Marido."

"We do," Nichols said and gave a short nod of his head as a greeting to Tom.

"Please sit down," Tom said. "Do you mind if I stay?"

"Please do," Nichols said, and we all sat down. Nichols and Young sat next to each other on the couch, and Tom picked the arm chair next to the window. I sat in a cushioned chair opposite the couch.

"What can we do for you?" I asked.

"We picked up Sanchez. He's on his way back here. The victim's wife is here now, too. Do you know her?" Nichols said.

I shook my head, but Tom replied that he did.

"A group of us were all assigned together in Spain, and then we crossed paths off and on again. Vince knows her the best."

"She's already made contact with him. Think there's more to that relationship?" Detective Young asked.

"I honestly don't know. The four of them were very close for a while, but I never noticed any animosity between Vince and Doug," Tom said.

"Has she been able to help you in the investigation?" I asked.

"Some. She's very familiar with the dispute with Eric Gamble and Bob Bishop. Surprisingly, she thought her husband ripped them off, too," Nichols said.

"Really," Tom said.

Nichols looked at him like he wanted to snap at him, but he continued talking. "She said it irritated her, but that Doug said the by-laws authorized him expenses, and since he did most the work, he had every right to finally pay himself for expenses."

"Did Sanchez run because he knew you were bringing Doug's wife here?" I asked.

"We didn't bring her here. She wanted to come. What do you know about her and Sanchez?"

"Nothing. Only connection I know was with the victim, not her, and I passed it along earlier. Doug had turned Bill in for drinking years ago just before he was supposed to fly. Hurt his career."

"Well, it still bothered Sanchez," Young said.

"Is that what she said?" Tom asked.

They ignored his question. Nichols took a small paper notebook out of his pocket and studied it for a few seconds.

"She knows most of you guys and considers you friends. She says she never heard of you, West."

"She hasn't."

"I recommended she stay away from this place and all of you, but she insists on talking to you all. She claims that most of you were good friends of Doug," Nichols said.

"She's staying at a nearby hotel, but we imagine she'll be over here later today or this evening. We're concerned about that," Young said.

"Think she'll try to take revenge on her own?"

"Wouldn't be the first time, Jim. We're also worried that if she gets too close to learning the identity of the killer, she may find herself in danger. Officer Strong will be staying in close touch with her, but that will only work as much as Mrs. Nelson allows," Nichols said.

"What does everyone think about Bill's running like he did?" Detective Young asked.

"We think he's an idiot," Tom said. "It makes him look guilty."

I nodded but didn't add anything.

"We need all of you to keep an eye on Mrs. Nelson. Jim, she may not want to talk to you, or she may look at you as a neutral party to whom she can talk. Either way, if any of you thinks she is in danger, let us know right away. Likewise, if she shares with you anything pertinent to this case, let us know right away," Nichols said.

"Can you both do that? Young asked.

"Yes," Tom said.

"We will. At our five-thirty meeting, we'll make sure everyone knows your concern with her safety," I said.

"Thanks, and Jim, do you want to press charges on that guy from last night? I'm not as tolerant as Louise," Nichols said.

"No, I'm good, and there really wasn't that much to it."

"He could've hurt you, though, and the next guy may not be as lucky."

"No, I'd rather not."

"Suit yourself," Nichols said, and the two detectives walked out of our room.

"What happened last night?" Tom asked.

"Ran into Louise's jealous boyfriend. We got into a little scuffle, but there wasn't much to it. Neither one of us got hurt, although I may have broken his nose."

Tom grinned. "Really?"

"Yes, but he did start it, and I tried to explain to him that he had it all wrong."

"That's when you hurt your arm?"

"I didn't hurt it. The jerk hit me with a wooden rolling pin, like those a baker might use."

"A rolling pin, ha, and they want to ban guns."

Chapter 21

Vivian Nelson sat on the couch with Vince Flores sitting next to her. She had been crying and held a small package of tissue on her lap. A number of the guys stood around her consoling her and expressing their sympathy. Tom went directly to her, while I found a chair to sit in. I could express my sympathy later.

"You all know Viv," Vince said after everyone had found their seats. "She wants to say a few things before we get started with our meeting."

Viv remained seated, looking around the room before she began talking. "While it's good to see so many faces of old friends, it's doesn't bring me any joy today. I need this to be over. I can't think straight. I can't grieve right. I don't feel like it's me in here." She tapped herself over her heart. "They tell me the killer has to be one of you in this room. I can't believe it. I know Doug wasn't perfect. I screamed at him for the way he treated you, Bob, and you, Eric. I know Bill hated him, but why would any of you want to kill him."

"I didn't," Bob said in a voice that I barely heard.

"I'm not saying you did. I have no idea at all who would've, but I need for the person to turn himself in. I need for this to be over."

"Why do you think Bill hated him?" Dick asked.

"He sent Doug a few emails in the past year. Nasty emails, accusing him of stealing from Bob and Eric, and for ruining his life. He still hasn't gotten over the drinking incident. I think the fallout with Bob and Eric reignited the hatred."

"We all believe Doug did the right thing back then," Bob said.

"Thanks, Bob. Listen, I believe Doug had changed a little in the past couple of years. Nothing big, but he has been more consumed with money. We never have had any financial problems. We're not rich, but we've always been comfortable. Has he started a new business venture with any of you?"

A murmur of "no's" sounded around the room.

"I saw him today. It was him, but it wasn't him. I wish I hadn't seen him. Now when I think of him, I see the face I saw today. I want to forget that face. I want to remember him the way he was. The smiling face I knew. Not the pale ghost I saw today." Her eyes teared up again. "Help me."

She stood up, looked around at everyone, and walked out of the room. Vince started to get up and follow her, but she looked back and motioned for him to stay.

I noticed a number of the guys were dabbing at their eyes with the backs of their hands. She had made an impression.

"I didn't expect that. That was quite moving," Tom said to me.

"Yes, it was."

"If any one of you killed Doug, have the balls, the backbone, the decency to turn yourself in. Tell us your side of the story. At least give us a chance to understand. Hell, we're supposed to be friends," Frank said.

Not surprisingly, no one confessed.

"Vince, has she shared anything with you that might indicate who the killer is?" Dick asked.

"No. Nothing at all."

"Someone needs to be in constant contact with her," Tom

said. "She may not be safe here."

"Listen to us. It's like we actually believe that one of us is a murderer," Ed White said. "I don't care what the police think. I can't believe one of us killed Doug. How can we all still be sitting here acting like friends if we believe one of us is a killer?"

"None of us is the type that cuts and runs, Ed," Frank said.

"So, which one of us killed him and why? Was it you, LG? Was he threatening to tell your wife about your concubine in Brazil?" Ed stressed the word concubine.

"Get with it, Ed, no one says concubine anymore," LG said, and everyone laughed.

"See. We make light of it, but none of us are asking the hard questions of each other. Not even our internet wonder Detective Imperious West. I thought you were supposed to solve this," Ed said.

I didn't answer him.

"How about you, Pete? Was there more to that dead girl in the Philippines than we all were told? Were you and Doug just having fun, and it just got out of hand?"

"Ed, you were there, too. You know we left that bar as a group hours before she was killed. Her death had nothing to do with any of us."

"Do I? And Larry, good old Larry, always trying to fly under the radar. Could any of those rumors be true? Did Doug try to blackmail you?" Ed appeared to be determined to accuse everyone, and despite his attitude, I hoped he continued.

"Oh, come on, Ed. I've been through that so many times, it only bores me these days. Now days I could care less if someone wants to think I'm gay. Hell, there's even some status in it in today's world."

"Ed, what are you trying to do?" Tom asked.

"What your friend is obviously too afraid to do. I'm trying to get the truth out in the open. We sit around like we're friends when we all have plenty of history. I remember when Doug and you, Frank, got into a fight in flight school."

"That's going way back. We were both drunk. The fight was broken up seconds after it started, and we were both laughing about it later that same night. He's twice my size. I still have no idea what caused me to attack him," Frank said.

"Perhaps you do remember, and it still bothers you," Ed said. "James and LG, you guys also fly AirExpress with him. Either of you bringing in drugs in your planes? Maybe Doug found out."

"Yep, that's it, you got me," James Streelman said.

"Okay, no drugs, but could there be other secrets you two don't want to have become public? We all know the rumors. And how about you two, Eric and Bob. Did both of you simply roll over and take the screwing Doug gave you? Or were one of you man enough to do something about it?"

"Are you done, Ed?" Pete asked. "You haven't included me, and we all know that last year he took my favorite hat right off my head and threw it into that lake."

"Somebody had to," Mike Powers said, and again everyone broke out into laughter. "Who wears a hat that says Stud."

"Make fun of all this. Someone else may die this week. I wonder who it will be?" Ed said and left the room.

The meeting broke up shortly afterwards. No prizes were announced, and it seemed to me the week itself was dying a slow death. The big dinner, scheduled for later that evening, never happened.

Tom and I walked over to the Waffle and Shakes restaurant.

"What's your take on what happened at the meeting?" he asked, as we sat down at a table.

"Strange, but I guess we should've expected something like that happening. The stress on everyone is building, and Vivian's speech ignited some feelings."

"They sure did. She's as pretty as I remember her. Almost as tall as us, still in great shape, and blue eyes that can look through you. I think her hair was lighter back then."

"Probably dyes it to hide the grey. She's at that age."

"That age? Thought you said you weren't an expert when it came to women."

"You got me there," I said.

Tom's phone rang. "Hey…... Waffle and Shakes…… sure."

"Someone joining us?" I asked.

"Yes. Viv and Vince."

"Interesting. Are you pretty sure the geographical separation has kept the two physically apart?"

"No, but I don't remember hearing anything from either Doug or Vince since we started coming here that the two have had any personal contact between trips," Tom said.

"Would you have remembered if you did?"

"Yes, because I've always been one that thought the four of them may have been involved in wife swapping. Always felt a little guilty for feeling that way, but I would have remembered if I heard anything that indicated the four were getting together again. Not that there's anything wrong with it."

"I wouldn't have been able to do it."

"Me neither," Tom said.

"I mean what do you say when you're driving home? How'd you sleep last night, honey?"

"Or how about if your wife says that she can't wait to do that again. It has to take a certain sort to be able to handle doing that."

"I guess we need to avoid the topic while they're here," I said.

Tom nodded and said, "Speak of the devil, here they are."

We stood up.

Chapter 22

Vivian Nelson hadn't changed clothes, but she had put on heels which I found interesting. She had on flats at the meeting not even an hour earlier. I noticed because one of them had a serious scuff mark on the toe. The scuff mark may have been the driving force behind the change of shoes, but I couldn't help but wonder if the high heels were for Vince's benefit. I forced that thought to the back of my mind. It wouldn't do any good to let my imagination go wild, and besides, what did I really know about women and their choice of footwear?

"Tom, Jim, thanks for letting us join you," Vince said.

"Yes, Tom, this was my idea when I heard you, Jim, were working with the police to help identify Doug's murderer," Viv said.

I didn't like the way that sounded. Everyone in the group should be working with the police to help identify the killer. Yet, I knew the reality of the situation. Most of the group would go home today if they could, and very few wanted to do anything at all with the police.

"Yes, I'm Jim West." I extended a hand. She took it. I noticed her hands were small and soft. Her finger nails covered in a clear gloss.

"Please sit down and join us," Tom said.

"Have you ordered?" Vince asked.

"No, still trying to decide," Tom said.

"Didn't know you had more than one choice here."

"Well, it's between the bacon waffle or the waffle covered with strawberries and whipped cream," I said.

"I'll just have a chocolate shake," Vivian said to Vince in a voice not much louder than a whisper.

The three of us all ordered the bacon waffle and different flavors of milk shakes. I went with chocolate chip.

"Jim, I asked Vince to bring me here so I could tell you what I've been thinking. Tom, you listen in, too. For the first two days, all I could think about was how terrible it was. Mostly, it was just self-pity. Of course, I felt sorry for him and our children. Our daughter has had to postpone her wedding, but mostly, I knew I was wallowing in my own self-pity."

"I told you, that's normal," Vince said.

She smiled at him and put her hand over his. "It may be, but yesterday I realized I had to do something to focus my mind outward. I began to think about how this could have happened. I know," she paused, and I thought she might tear up, "I knew Doug better than anyone. He's been a great husband and father and very nice to people. But he has this thing about money that has become worse the last couple of years."

"What do you mean?" Tom asked.

"He doesn't mind spending it, don't get me wrong, but he kept coming up with get rich quick ideas. Most of them were a touch on the shady side, and you know, it was absolutely stupid, because we didn't need the money. The issue with Eric and Bob was a perfect example. He never would have done that when he was younger. For whatever reason, he thought he deserved the biggest part of the pie."

"And not just by a small amount, he wanted a large extra slice," Vince said.

"When did you learn this?" I asked.

"Today," Vince said.

"Yes, I told him all this today. Doug sued our favorite diner a few months ago for finding a hair on his plate. This place is a dive, but we both loved going there. We always laughed that the place had to be bribing someone to stay open. A hair on a plate was nothing, but he sued saying it was a quick, easy way to make a little money, because the restaurant and its insurance would want to make a quick and quiet settlement. They did, but it was a couple thousand dollars we didn't need, and now we can't go back."

"He started bringing expensive booze back from overseas by the case and selling it to his cousin who owns a liquor store. He'd clear a couple hundred dollars and for what? He would've never done that in the old days."

"Something in Doug's brain must have shorted out, because the Doug we know never would've violated the rules like that," Vince said.

"That does sound strange," Tom said.

"I did tell the police to look hard at Bill. He sent a couple of real nasty emails to Doug after the situation with Eric and Bob blew up. But afterwards, something Detective Nicklaus said to me on the phone got me to thinking."

"It's Detective Nichols, Viv, not Nicklaus," Vince said.

She ignored him. "He said the messages appeared to be more like angry venting and accusatory than threatening. Thinking back, he's probably right. The emails didn't say anything like I'm going to kill you or someone's going to kill you one day."

"About a month ago, Doug told me he was going into a new business venture with someone. He didn't tell me who, and I believe the reason he didn't was because I gave him such a hard time about his handling of his business with Eric and Bob. I didn't think much more about it until yesterday as I was preparing to come here. I remembered he made a statement that with any luck, this trip would pay for itself."

"Like someone here might pay for his trip," Vince said.

She nodded. "But I have no idea who or why."

"No one has talked about a new business relationship with Doug," Tom said.

"That might be because of the bad ending to his prior one," Vince said,

"Or because there was something not quite legal with this new one," I said.

"Interesting," Tom said.

"But why would you kill someone who you are just getting started with in a business? Why not just not agree to it in the first place?" I said, but I already had an answer or two bouncing around in my head.

"I know it doesn't make sense, but he said it, and it had to be with one of us. I mean he was only coming here to be with us. There's no other connection you or he had with Myrtle Beach, right?" Vince said.

"That's right, none at all."

"Does he share with you his business finances?" I asked.

"He did in the past, but not with this one. I thought it was because of the hard time I gave him over the last venture. Of course, it could've simply been that the business hadn't yet gotten off its feet."

"Does he use your family money to start up the businesses?" I asked.

"He has in the past, but in this case, he indicated there were minimal startup costs. He evaded giving me any details which made me suspicious."

"You think that business may be behind what happened here?"

"Jim, I don't know, but the more I think about it, the more certain I get that it was. He flew straight here, and his return trip was taking him straight back home. Whatever he was setting up or had set up was going to happen here."

"Have you told the police?"

"Yes, and they seemed interested."

"As they should be," Vince said.

"I've authorized the police to go through all my, our, phones and computers. Can you do something more, Jim?"

"Not really, the police wouldn't like me conducting formal interviews or searches. All the guys know they can come to me with anything, and they know anything I get, I share with the police."

"Are you like a deputy?"

"No, more like a conduit the guys can use if they're hesitant to go directly to the police." I felt like saying more like a "stuck-ee", since this wasn't something for which I volunteered.

"Well, I appreciate it. Detective Nichols," she glanced at Vince to make sure she had the name right, "said they would try to discover who his new business partner was. I would think someone else might know, even if it was something shady."

"Like bringing drugs in from Asia or South America," Tom said.

"I can't believe that's anything he would do. Doug has always, always been a stickler for following the rules."

"Except for the alcohol," I said.

"Yes, that's true, but he did some research and always kept the amount he snuck back below the amount that would warrant anything more than a fine. It was so stupid. He made a pittance for taking a risk that could have gotten him fired. Other than that, I never knew him to break any rules when it came to his job. Did you?" she asked Vince.

"No, of course not, but we need to talk to LG. He knew him best with AirExpress. Both Jim and James, too, but I don't think any of them ever flew together."

"I imagine the police will do that," I said.

"Maybe we should, too," Vince said.

I started to say that we ought to leave the interviews to the police, but I wondered if they shook the proverbial tree a little, something might fall out.

"He did that to you, too," Viv said.

I touched my bandage. "Yes."

"He's afraid of you."

"If so, he's overinflated my abilities."

"I wonder."

Our meals arrived, and for a while, conversation was limited. Viv asked Tom about his wife, and the two talked about their past lives in the air force.

I thought about the new information concerning Doug and the new business opportunity. A couple of possibilities had popped into my mind when Viv mentioned that it didn't require any startup funds. As a pilot traveling international routes, he might be agreeing to transport something for a payment. Something that AirExpress wouldn't know about and likely illegal. It would have to be more than doing something simple for a friend.

Perhaps one of the other AirExpress pilots knew something, but if it was illegal why would they ever admit to it. Why would they pay him to do something they could do themselves? That left someone else in the group. It also opened up a dozen other scenarios. None of them, however, warranted killing Doug.

Another idea had taken root in my mind, too. What if Doug had planned on blackmailing someone over some piece of information he had? Blackmail is risky. Doug's death would be proof of that, so why take on such a scheme? All I could think of was that it fit in with his desire for quick, easy money, and he may never have taken a serious look at the risk.

A long shot, I knew, and I couldn't see how any of these middle age, middle class men would have anything in their lives blackmailable. However, that was the point of the blackmail, having knowledge of some deep, dark, hidden secret that the target did not want to have disclosed. I didn't think I had anything like that, but I imagined some people would.

"I also want to clear the air about something, Jim," Viv said.

"Yes?"

"The police asked me about it, so I should mention it to you. There was never anything really true with the husband swapping rumors of old. We both can see why they may have started, and some of our past activities may have come close," she paused and smiled at Vince. He visibly blushed.

"I appreciate you volunteering this, but whether or not, and I'm not arguing with what you said, I can't see how the past could be the motive behind the murder. The motive would be if Vince thought Doug's death might result in you becoming his prize."

"Becoming his prize. What an interesting way to say it. Vince hasn't had any direct communication with me for a year, and even that was two minutes on Doug's phone last year while they were here. Doug had called while the two were together, and I asked if I could say hello. So, if Vince had his sights set on me, he's not been very open about it."

"Let me jump in here, Viv. Our past has nothing to do with Doug's murder. I swear that to you. By the way, I'm happily married, but Viv would be a prize, a grand prize, for anyone. It's just that I'm not looking," Vince said.

"No one's accusing you," Tom said.

"I brought it up, Vince," Viv said, and gave his hand a squeeze.

"I know, but to make our past a reason for me to kill Doug today is ridiculous."

I thought of the quote "Thou protest too much." It probably came from some Shakespeare play, but I've known it to be true. Sometimes, the guilty try too hard to convince others of their innocence and only draw more attention to themselves. In this case, though, I didn't think their past had anything to do with Doug's murder.

Chapter 23

Louise called me that evening and explained that she had an appointment with Viv, so we wouldn't need to get together. She said Viv had called after eating dinner with me and said she wanted to talk. I asked if Vince was going to be there, and Louise said no. This was just going to be the two of them.

That explained why less than five minutes after the call with Louise ended, Vince came to our hotel suite with a bottle of Jeremiah Weed. I knew the bottle of Weed meant some serious drinking lay ahead, but I didn't plan to be part of it.

I had an initial shot before complaining about my head hurting and heading to my room. They didn't seem to mind. I heard the sound of someone else arriving and the tinkling of glasses touching together for one toast after another. The suite got noisy with laughter, cussing, and the occasional toast "To Doug!"

They broke up less than an hour later, the bottle presumably empty. Tom knocked on my door.

"Are you awake?'

"Yes, come in." I sat up on my bed and set my kindle on the nightstand.

"Sorry about the noise. Vince texted Mike who came over and joined us." His voice had a slight slur, and he had a tight grip on the door frame.

"I wondered who it was."

"You could've stayed out there with us."

"I know, but you guys didn't need me there."

Tom nodded and grinned. "Guess what?"

"Before Mike showed up, Vince said the four of them used to skinny dip together. They would play games and roughhouse, and he admitted there was a lot of touching, but he said they had an agreement."

"An agreement?" I asked. Tom seemed to have lost his train of thought.

"A code, that was the word he used. No sex. They had their own wives for that."

"Romantic," I said, being a little sarcastic.

"Yeah, I guess it was, but I couldn't have handled it."

"Are you going to be able to play golf in the morning?"

"Sure, I've been worse. Good night." He closed my door, and I went back to my reading. A few minutes later, I turned off my light and tried to go to sleep. The last sound I remember hearing before falling asleep was Tom throwing up in our shared bathroom.

The next morning on the first tee box, significant grumbling about continuing the tournament began.

"They've arrested Bill and Doug is gone, doesn't it seem like we shouldn't be doing this anymore," Larry said to the group.

"I have to be at the police station at two, so I don't care if we play or not. I just want this to be over and to go back to Asheville," Ed said.

"We can cancel the scramble on Saturday, but let's at least get through today and tomorrow," Dick said.

"That's only because you're in first place. I agree with Larry, we should call the rest of the week off in respect of Doug. With Viv being here, I feel even more guilty continuing to play," Streelman said.

"Don't make Vivian's arrival an excuse to stop playing. She doesn't want us to stop. I asked her," Vince said.

"Still, it's a valid consideration. Some people may think we're not sensitive. I, for one, however, agree with Dick. Let's play through tomorrow," Frank said.

"Well, we're here, so I'm teeing off," Pete said.

He and Eric were in the same cart, and I saw Eric motion ahead. The cart moved up next to the white tees. Frank and Tom pulled up next to them. I heard more grumbling, but the other carts lined up behind them.

Scheduled in what was supposed to be the last foursome, James Streelman and I shared a cart, waiting for the groups ahead of us to move out of range.

"This sucks. There are only two of us, they should've let us tee off first," he said.

"You're right. Maybe we can kill some time by practicing our putting after we finish each hole."

"We could except this group will likely be right on our tail."

I looked back and saw a group of eight golfers waiting for us to tee off. "Maybe their first foursome will be really slow."

"We'll see."

Not only were they not slow, they could hit the ball a mile. More than once, they hit their shots into us despite the distance between us and them. The first time, neither one of us made a big deal about. The second time, Streelman shouted back at them.

"They're so far away, I doubt if they can hear you. That drive must have been over three hundred yards." We had just hit our second shots up to a long par five and were driving toward the green when one of their golf balls landed about fifteen feet to our right. It bounced along with us for another twenty yards.

"I'm more impressed that he hit in the fairway," Streelman said.

We were both short of the green lying two. Our third shots landed solidly on the green and after two putting, we both walked away with a par.

"You know, we're both playing pretty good, so far," I said.

"Don't jinx it by saying so far. That's just anticipating some lousy play. Anticipating it will make it happen."

I was considering my response when a golf ball landed on the green. We were off to the side and behind the hole. A few seconds later another ball landed short but rolled up close to the hole. A third ball landed on the edge of the green, rolling just off onto the fringe. We didn't see the fourth shot, but we guessed it may have landed before the others somewhere off the green.

"These guys are really good," I said.

We rode off and had no more contact with them until the eleventh hole. A three-hundred-and-thirty-yard par four, we were both putting when a ball rolled up close to us on the green.

"That's it! I'm picking that ball up," Streelman said.

"Let it be. That was his tee shot. He probably just hit the shot of his life."

"The game can't be fun when you're that good," he said.

We left the ball on the green. Just after teeing off on the next hole, a golf cart pulled up next to us with two young guys on it.

"Hey, we're sorry about hitting into you. We're just playing great today. Everything is going longer," the driver said.

"And straighter," the other player said.

"That's okay. Just give us a little more distance," I said.

"We will. Again, sorry about that," the driver said.

The two of us settled into a groove, playing a lot better than usual. James started telling me about himself. I didn't know him that well, and he had always been a bit aloof. However, parring four holes in a row can do a lot for one's spirit.

On the seventeenth hole, I brought up Doug's murder. At first, he answered me with few words, like he really wasn't listening to me. However, when I mentioned that two of the guys suggested I talk to him about Doug, I got a real reaction.

"What? Who said what? I don't know anything about Doug's death."

"They just said since you've flown in and out of South America with AirExpress, like Doug, you may know something."

"We never flew together. What did they imply?"

"Nothing. I wanted to learn a little more about Doug, and they said I should talk to you. Seemed logical to me when they said it." I thought Streelman was overreacting and wondered if that was his natural behavior, or if I had hit a nerve.

"He was a friend, a pilot with AirExpress, and a mediocre golfer. That's all I know."

"His wife says he was hoping to start a business with one of the guys here. Any idea who?"

"After what he did to Eric and Bob, I don't think anyone would go into business with him. I know I wouldn't."

"It may not have been an actual business. May not have even been totally legal, but he gave her the impression that whatever he was doing might pay for his golf trip here."

Streelman didn't respond, but I could see a vein in his temple swell, and his face became taut. He parked the cart next to the green and got out. He missed a four-foot par putt, and wouldn't make eye contact with me when we got back into the cart.

We played the last hole in silence, and maybe because our

rhythm had been disrupted, we both scored poorly on the last hole. He annotated our double bogeys before giving me the scorecard.

"You know, you're an ass," he said as we headed back to the clubhouse.

Chapter 24

I grabbed a hotdog and a Yuengling draft for lunch. Everyone else had their lunch or were already getting ready to leave. The mood of the group gave me the impression the golf week was dying a quick death.

Normally we would sit with the foursome with whom we played, if we weren't all sitting together at some large table or two. Looking around, I saw our gang scattered throughout the room. Streelman pulled a chair up to a small table where Larry and Ed were drinking beer. The stacked plates on the table indicated they had already finished lunch.

I sat down at an empty table. What had I said that irritated Streelman so much? His behavior made me suspicious of him, but was that simply a reaction that could be rationalized? He fit the size of the person who attacked me, but so did eleven others. I didn't see a lot of my attacker, but did his eyes match? A good question, however the attack happened in near dark. I couldn't swear to much more than my attacker had two eyes.

I needed to talk to LG next. He also flew with AirExpress, and even though I had talked with him briefly before, he might be able to shed some light on Streelman, too. I saw LG stand up with a group about to leave.

"Why are you all by yourself? Have a bad day?" Tom asked. He sat down next to me.

"You look like you're ready to leave," I said, taking a bite of my hotdog.

"I am, but finish your lunch. This crowd has me depressed, and my game didn't help. How'd you do?"

"For the most part I played well. Broke ninety, and that's my goal. Had a group behind us that should be on the tour. On eleven or twelve, a three-hundred-and-thirty-yard hole, one of their tee shots rolled up next to us as were putting."

"Damn, love to be able to do that."

"Me, too. So how has this crowd got you depressed?"

"I don't know, but it has. It's like Doug's death has only just now sunk in. It's also like Viv's arrival has spooked everyone, and they all want to avoid what may happen next."

"Anything specific?" I asked.

"No, but if we get everyone to come back and play tomorrow to at least finish out the team competition, I'll be surprised."

"That's too bad."

"People are starting to turn on each other, too. Larry, Ed, James, and Bill want to quit now, and they're pissed that the others want to play one more day. We already agreed to skip Saturday's scramble, so I thought that would be a good compromise."

"I hit a nerve with Streelman today," I said.

"I'm guessing not with a golf ball."

"No, we were actually getting along fine, and then on seventeen, I mentioned that a couple of the guys suggested I talk to him about Doug. When he said that he didn't know why, I mentioned about them both flying into South America with AirExpress. I also mentioned that Doug had made the comment that he had a business deal or concept that he thought would pay him enough to cover this golf trip."

"How'd he react?"

"He got real tense. Blood vessels popping out of his head, and clammed up."

"Sounds like you did hit a nerve," Tom said.

"Yes, but was it something illegal they were planning, and was his reaction because of that, or is there more to it?" Or did I think I saw more there than there was? Either way he stopped talking to me."

"Want me to talk to him?"

"If you want to. He may open up to you if it's only something that he's embarrassed about. I think the police will be interviewing him again based on what Viv has already told them. After all, only LG and him fly AirExpress."

"No, Jim M also does. I'll try to get to Streelman right after we get back," Tom said.

"May be a good idea. I plan on talking to LG."

We left the clubhouse and drove back to our hotel. I wanted to get in touch with Louise and ensure the police were aware of Streelman's reaction.

"You know, I heard once a few years back, some of the international crews would bring back foreign currencies and then sell them to people going overseas at a rate better than the banks, but they could still make a small profit," Tom said.

"I can't imagine that would be very profitable," I said. "There's a spot," I pointed at an empty parking spot in the garage.

"No, I can't either. I think they do it mostly to help their friends and friends' friends. You know, Streelman may have thought you were trying to accuse him."

"Maybe." I hoped LG could shed some light on the matter, but I had talked to him a number of times already and hadn't learned much.

I found him stretched out on a lounge chair on the beach behind the hotel. He was wearing a rather small bathing suit. I hadn't known any of the guys to use the beach, since most felt it was still too cool to go swimming.

"Hey, LG, you're going to get burned."

He looked over at me and grinned, "Heard you were looking for me." He must have noticed my look of curiosity and raised his cell phone in his left hand. "Jim M warned me he told you where I was. Here to do a citizen's arrest?"

"For wearing that suit, maybe."

He grinned. "My wife says I'm too tall to wear this."

"I think it's okay with tall just not fat."

"First warm sunny afternoon without a cold breeze this week. What can I do for you, special agent?"

I sat down on the dry sand next to him. "I'm trying to figure out a motive. We all had the opportunity and the weapon, but why would someone want Doug dead?"

"Can't help you there, Jim."

"Viv says that Doug had told her right before coming here that he was working on another business matter with one of us in the group. He said that it might provide him with enough profit to cover the expenses of this trip."

"Can't believe anyone would go into business with him after the fiasco with Bob and Eric."

"That's what she told him, too. She said he wouldn't elaborate on the business or say who his partner or partners might be."

"So, you think he might have been killed over this business?"

"I have no idea and was wondering if you've heard any rumors about any smuggling or other criminal activity that other AirExpress crews may have gotten involved in? Could he have been trying to set something illegal up?"

"Not to my knowledge. I got along fine with Doug, but I never flew with him in AirExpress or overlapped with him anywhere."

"I asked the same questions with Streelman today, and he got mad, overreacted. Any idea why he may have?"

"No, although he's an emotional guy. He can get mad quicker than most, but professionally, he doesn't break the rules."

"His reaction struck me as odd, that's all. I didn't accuse him of anything, I just mentioned the supposed business matter and wanted to know if he had any knowledge of it."

"Can't help you there. Here, Jim, use my towel, take off your shirt, lay down, and catch some rays. We've got a half hour before we'll need to go up."

The sun did feel warm. For the most part the beach was quiet. I took off my shirt and stretched out on the towel.

"Did you get those scars in the war?"

"No. Those all came after I retired for sticking my nose in where it didn't belong."

"Like this?"

"Yes, just like this."

As I lay there in the sun, two older teenage girls ran past. Despite the cool air, both wore swimming suits that revealed more than they hid. They ran into the ocean just far enough to get their legs wet before turning around and sprinting back past us, laughing all the way. One of the girls' swimming suits had oblong openings cut into the sides of the top piece of the suit clearly revealing the outer sides of each breast.

"Oh, to be young again," LG said.

"Those looked like the suit came with those holes."

"My mom would've whipped my sister if she wore anything

like that. Those two couldn't have been more than teenagers."

"Late teens from the look of them. Their moms may not even know they have those suits," I said.

"Pretty blue color though," LG said and grinned.

Chapter 25

Guilt and fear are strong emotions that feast on most people. There are those who seem to have no emotions, but most normal humans have a hard time overcoming their fears or guilt. People who grow up with a fear of the dark, even as adults, will feel a sudden panic when the lights go out unexpectedly at night. Snakes, spiders, and even other things that crawl around on the floor, walls, and, heaven forbid, on the ceiling above you at night can bring out strong emotions from people of all ages.

Captophobia is an anxiety disorder and is the term for the fear of getting caught. It affects most people to some degree. I remembered the term from a couple classes I had long ago on reading body language. In some ways, it's what makes a polygraph effective.

Guilt can also cause significant anxiety in most people. Knowing you did something, even inadvertently, that caused some tragedy can haunt you for the rest of your life. Even doing something on purpose, that you know you shouldn't have done, can result in lingering guilt. Many people can't hold it in and will ultimately confess to someone.

The behavior and responses to these feelings vary from person to person, but it was this line of thinking that had me wondering more about Streelman's reaction while we waited for our five thirty meeting to get started. He didn't show up, and neither did Larry or Ed. The police had Bill come in for additional questioning, too.

"Any idea where everyone is?" Dick asked.

"Larry and Ed are packing. They're leaving in the morning," Frank said.

"Streelman?" Dick asked.

"The police came and picked him up," Vince said.

"Did they arrest him?" Pete asked.

"No, I believe they just took him to be interviewed," Vince said.

"How's Viv?" Mike asked.

"Hanging in there," Vince said.

The meeting didn't last long. After a short debate, the group agreed to play one more day to finish off the team competitions. No one hung around to chat afterwards.

"I want to say this has been a wasted week, but that sounds disrespectful and selfish," Tom said when we got back to the room.

"It's a natural reaction. No one is happy about being involved in all this."

"That's for sure. Everyone's dirty laundry gets exposed. Even the innocent."

"Luckily my life has been boring," I said.

"How can you say that? You've been involved in a number of murder investigations, found a missing person or two, and who knows what else."

"I mean my personal life."

"Same here, although I don't doubt that I've said some things and even done a few things that might not be considered politically correct," Tom said.

"Who hasn't?"

My phone buzzed, and I saw I had a text from Louise. "May I come up?"

"It's Louise. She wants to come up. Is that okay with you?"

Tom grinned. "Is the sky blue?"

"Sure, come up," I texted back.

The knock on the door came almost instantly after I sent the text.

Tom beat me to the door and let her in. She looked great. Dressed in white slacks and a turquoise blouse that was a tad bit tight on her, she definitely had Tom's attention.

"Officer Strong, how are you doing?" he asked.

"Good, and you two?

"Fine," we both said.

"I hope I'm not bothering you, but I talked to Vivian and she said she had already talked to everyone and then separately to you two."

"Yes, she did," Tom said. He definitely wanted the lead in this conversation.

"James Streelman has become a person of interest but is refusing to say anything to Detective Nichols. We're not inclined to point a finger at him or Sanchez, but their behavior is making them look very suspicious."

"We know," Tom said, although I wondered if he really did.

"We hear that a couple of the guys are leaving in the morning." She looked at me like she wondered why I hadn't told her about them. "Larry Brown and Edward White."

"They might wait until after we play in the morning and then leave," Tom said.

"Either of those two have any anger issues with Doug?"

"No," Tom said.

I shook my head when she looked at me.

"Cat got your tongue?"

I smiled. "No. Tom's doing good."

"Do you mind if I talk to Tom alone?"

That surprised me, but I didn't object. The two of them stepped out onto the balcony. I sat down on the couch and watched. She leaned slightly against the balcony railing and stood slightly more erect. Her blouse seemed to stretch a little more. I looked at Tom. If he was a puppy, one of his hind legs would be bouncing up and down right about now. He didn't have a chance. She smiled and laughed at something he said.

Starting to feel like a voyeur, I went to the kitchen and grabbed a beer. Someone knocked on the door to our hotel room, and when I opened it, I found Edward White standing there alone. At first, he stared at me, motionless, but then he reached out and tried to grab hold of the front of my shirt. I sensed that he had been drinking and had little trouble brushing his hand away. His aggressive behavior continued, and he took a couple of quick steps toward me, forcing me to back away.

"What's up Ed?"

"You caused all this," spittle actually shot out of his mouth. "Don't come back next year or ever. If you do, I'll finish the job on you." His eyes shot up at my bandaged forehead.

He tried to grab my shirt again, wobbling a little as he did so. This time I lifted my forearm between us. He grabbed it and held on, making me wonder if the need to hold onto something to steady himself was just as much of a need as his attempt to intimidate me.

"You're trying to frame one of us!"

"No, I'm not." I kept my voice down as a counter to his shouting.

"Bullshit! That's what OSI does, and that's what you're doing here. I think I might just kick your ass."

"Ed, what are you doing?" Tom said.

"Let go of him," Louise said. They had come in from the balcony and could see us from the living room.

Ed let go of my arm and took a couple of unsteady steps backwards. "You're both just helping him."

"We're trying to find out who murdered your friend," Louise said. "You should be helping us, too."

Ed turned around and left.

"Did he hit you?" Tom asked.

"No. I think he's been drinking and worked up enough courage to come here to vent some of his anger."

"We heard him threaten you. Want me to go arrest him? Might make him think twice before he does something like that again."

"No. I think he's harmless," I said, but I did wonder about his remark about finishing the job. Had he been the one who attacked me? He was the right size, but beyond that I had no other reason to think he committed either crime.

"Could he have been the one?" Louise asked me, as though she could read my thoughts.

"Possibly, but for some reason, I want to say no."

Chapter 26

"You want to stay an extra week?" Tom asked after Louise left. She had stayed for another fifteen minutes after Ed left. While the conversation mostly focused on the investigation, Tom did his best to steer it around to be about Louise. To my surprise, she opened up to him a little. Not that she said anything to him that I didn't already know.

"Sorry, no, and I don't see how you can either."

"I know. I might move here. You notice how her eyes twinkle when she smiles or laughs?"

"Actually, I have," I said.

"I think I'm besmitten. That's the right word, right?"

"I don't know, but I don't think people actually say it anymore."

"I think she likes you. I asked her if you and her were a thing –"

Interrupting, I said, "You mean a besmitten thing?"

He grinned. "Yes, and all she said was that you were leaving in two days. You know like the answer was yes but no."

"I do like her, but like she said, I'm leaving. There's no future for us. Besides, I've got a partner already."

"A partner? Who came up with that term? Sounds like a sidekick or a buddy. Something between a paramour and a squeeze. Are you going steady? Besides in many societies it is normal and expected for the man to have many other women."

"I thought you were interested in her."

"I am. It just frustrates me that we have all these moral codes when it comes to love. Don't get me wrong. I do not want to leave my wife or have her leave me, but I think when I'm away it ought to be okay for me to seek the pleasures of another woman."

"You ought to write romance novels," I said.

"I can't spell."

Another knock on the door saved me from more of his rambling conversation.

We let Dick Leyes into the room and offered him a beer. After we all had one, we sat around the small table.

"Did Ed cause any trouble when he was here?" Dick asked.

"Not really," I said.

"Good. He's not at his best. Been drinking too much and being obnoxious. Someone mentioned he had come here to teach you a lesson. His words not mine. Then I heard the police woman was here and wondered what all happened. Ed didn't kill Doug, because he was with me for most of the late afternoon."

"You've told the police that," I said.

"Yes, but they kept pressing on the possibility he was out of my sight for thirty minutes. I told them I didn't think so, but I couldn't swear to it."

"Ed came here and threatened me, but that was all."

"Okay, good. Well, it's not good, but you understand. He can be an ass, but I've known him forever, and he's not really a bad guy. He might forget how many strokes he had on a hole or two, but I've never known him to do anything seriously wrong."

"Looks like the killer may get away with it," Tom said.

"Possibly, but it seems like the tension is rising. That can cause people to make mistakes," I said.

"Like Ed coming here," Dick said.

"Exactly. I think the police are interviewing a number of us today. We've all been interviewed before. My guess is they are trying to shake the tree very hard to rattle the killer. Sometimes it works," I said.

"They expect him to run?" Tom asked.

"To do something," I said.

"Let's hope he doesn't hurt someone else," Tom said.

"Why would he hurt someone now?" Dick said.

"I don't know, but whoever it is killed Doug and then tried to kill Jim. He's certainly not acting like a sane person," Tom said.

"That's true," Dick said.

"I know it doesn't make sense, but our killer may start feeling trapped or cornered. He shouldn't, because we really don't have a clue, but in his mind the more pressure that is put on him, the more he may think the police are closing in. Whatever his secrets are, he starts to worry that others are about to uncover them," I said.

"Is that why he attacked you, Jim?" Dick asked.

"I think so. He had some crazy idea I could identify him as the killer. He panicked then and may do so again."

"You mean attack you?" Tom asked.

"No, no not that. I meant that he might panic again and do something foolish."

"Like Bill. He tried to run away."

"That's right, Dick, like Bill. He put himself under the microscope when he ran, and he ran because he knew he had written those emails to Doug and thought the police might find out. Of course, they did."

"Why doesn't he just give himself up?" Tom asked.

"Who knows? He might. Some do. Some also commit suicide,

leaving a long note behind. It intrigues me that there may still be a motive out there that hasn't come to light. If it has, no one has recognized it as such," I said.

"It had to be pretty significant if it caused him to murder Doug," Tom said.

"Yeah, something that would ruin his life. It couldn't just be that Doug tried to rip him off. The thing is we know each other. Someone else here would know the secret. Hell, we all know a few things about each other that we might be ashamed of today, but none of them are worth killing over and all of them are known to more than one person. We talk, maybe I should say gossip about each other all the time, and we all know that we do," Dick said.

"It could be a crime of passion, you know a spur of the moment thing," Tom said.

"Possibly, we don't know what transpired in the last few minutes between Doug and his killer."

"What are you two saying? That there might have been something romantic going on between the two? That's crap," Dick said.

"No, nothing like that. Crime of passion simply means it wasn't premeditated. It occurred because of a sudden explosion of emotions," I said.

"Still can't see that. We have a few hot heads, but they're not the killing type," Dick said.

I resisted the urge to ask him how he knew that. Most people if pushed hard enough can become violent, especially if they already have a weapon in their hand. But I also knew there was a large step between becoming violent and killing someone.

"So, what do we have? Did Doug know something that would

utterly destroy the killer's life and was blackmailing him?" I asked the question to get a suspicion I had had for the last two days out into the open.

"Like what?" Tom asked.

"It would have to be something huge; something no one else knows about," Dick said.

"Since you know most of each other's secrets, it's likely something recent."

"Like he killed or raped someone," Dick said.

"Not likely, and how would Doug have found out about it?"

"Yeah, Doug didn't live close to any of us. How could he know what we were doing? I don't see how he could know much," Tom said.

"Then we aren't making much progress," Dick said.

"But the facts still remain, someone killed Doug and later attacked me. That person had to have had a motive."

"We know why he went after you, but why Doug?" Tom said.

"We're back to square one," I said.

Another knock on the door interrupted us. I opened it to find Detective Young and Officer Whip Miller there.

"May we come in?" Young asked.

"Sure," I said.

He didn't seem to be surprised to see Dick with us. I offered them a soft drink, but Young declined for both of them.

"I won't be long. I'm here to give you one more chance to come clean with us. Spill any and all the dirt you have on each other now and avoid the embarrassment of us digging it up with your friends and family back at your homes," Young said.

"What do you mean?" Tom asked.

"It means we are about to send out a lengthy set of

investigative leads to your hometown police departments asking for a full scrutiny of your lives. You, too, West."

"That doesn't make sense," Tom said.

"Can you do that?" Dick asked.

"Of course," Young said. "Someone has to have a nasty little secret, and we intend to find out what it is."

"If you find out something exciting about me, please let me know. I could use an ego boost after this week," Tom said.

"This is not funny," Miller said.

"We know that," I said.

Miller looked at me with a stare that I guessed he thought might intimidate me.

"We're talking to everyone tonight to let you know when you get home you might be the topic of conversation for a while. Any rumors about you before may become a little more widespread now. Same at your work," Young said.

"That's not fair," Dick said.

"If you're innocent and have nothing to hide, then there's nothing to worry about," Young said.

I knew that wasn't true. I'd been involved several investigations in the past wherein digging into people's background uncovered a variety of embarrassing things unrelated to the investigation. No one's perfect, and most of us have a few things in our past that we'd rather keep secret. A friend of mine almost got divorced because five years earlier at a crazy party where everyone had too much to drink, he and a married woman got into a heavy session of kissing and petting. It never progressed past that, and there had been no further sexual activity between the two. Years later, when the same woman and her husband fought each other in a nasty divorce, the husband's lawyer uncovered the incident that then became very public. That disclosure almost wrecked my friend's marriage.

"Now's your last chance to tell us what you know. If we solve the case, we won't have to go digging into your past," Young said.

None of us had anything to add.

Chapter 27

"What was that all about?" Dick asked after the police left. "Like we said, I believe they're trying to ratchet up the pressure on the killer. Whatever motivated him to kill Doug may be something he doesn't want to become public knowledge. The police want him to overreact and do something that will implicate himself."

"Yeah, we talked about that before," Tom said. We had.

"Think it will work, Jim?" Dick asked.

"Maybe, we know the fear of the police finding out about Bill's emails to Doug is what made him try to leave."

"But our killer hasn't panicked yet," Tom said.

"No, but now he has to know his past is going to go under the microscope. Any hope that his secret will remain a secret may start to fade."

"He might've thought that making it to the end of the week and leaving Myrtle Beach may put an end to it all. Now he might not be so sure," Dick said.

"Exactly," I said.

"I've done a few things I'd like to keep hidden, but nothing that I would kill over. Everyone does. Remember those parties in Vegas?" Dick said.

"I claim alcohol poisoning as my defense," Tom said. "My wife, our wives would have killed us if they had known."

"Yeah, but neither of us did anything that bad, did we?" Dick asked.

"If we had, we wouldn't remember anyway because of all the alcohol we drank. Lucky we survived."

They both laughed.

"I think I almost became an alcoholic during that assignment. I don't think I did, but sin city didn't get its name for nothing."

"Glad I wasn't there," I said.

"We thought it was fun at the time," Dick said and shook his head. "If I could live those years over again, I would definitely not go to a single one of those parties."

"Yes, you would. They were almost like squadron functions. We all went," Tom said.

"We'd all be kicked out of the air force in today's world," Dick said.

"And deservedly so," Tom said.

"The air force changed a lot from when we first got in, and from what I've been told it was a lot looser before us," I said.

"I think everything changed when they started letting women into the military," Tom said.

"We had to clean up our act a little bit. That's for sure." Dick said.

I felt like reminding them that women had served in the military for a long time before we joined, but I knew they meant as pilots in their fighter squadrons. To them, that was the air force.

Dick left a little later, and Tom went to his room to read. I sent Louise a text asking her how her day went. When I didn't get a quick reply, I imagined she might have joined Detective Nichols to interview some of the group.

Another knock on the door broke the silence in the room. Mike, Pete, and Frank stood there with two large pizza boxes.

"Dinner time," Frank said.

Mike followed Frank into the room, carrying a twelve pack of Yuengling. Pete carried a wad of napkins.

"This is to celebrate the last time we'll be interviewed by the police," Mike said.

"Yeah, we think they're done with us now," Pete said.

"Too bad the killer will get away with this. A blemish on your good record, Jim," Frank said.

"Hardly. I have a brain injury excuse." I tapped my bandage.

"Are they going to look at that before you go home?" Mike asked.

"Tomorrow, after golf."

"We'll be lucky if we can make up two foursomes tomorrow," Frank said.

"It's one of my favorite courses. We'll be there," Tom said.

My phone buzzed as a new text came in. James Streelman asked me if I could meet him in front of the hotel for a minute. He said it was urgent and asked me to come alone.

"Louise get back to you?" Tom asked.

"No, Streelman wants to meet me for a second downstairs."

"Streelman? Want someone to go with you?" Frank asked.

"No need. We'll just be out front. I shouldn't be long. I guess there's no chance a piece of pizza will be left over."

No one offered to save any. I left, regretting I didn't invite James up. Despite the growing darkness, the hotel security lights provided plenty of light to the small parking lot directly in front of the hotel. James leaned against a car that I figured was his.

"What's up?"

"I need to talk to you." His voice sounded stressed.

"Okay. I'm listening."

He looked up, and I followed his gaze. I didn't see anything but the front of the building. So much for my protection team, I thought.

"No, not here. Get in."

"James, I'm not going anywhere. There's pizza waiting for me upstairs. I'm willing to listen to you, but I'm not leaving. Come up and have some pizza with us."

"You don't understand. I plan on killing myself tonight, and I need someone to tell my story to. I need you to explain it to my wife after I'm gone."

"You can tell her yourself. And don't be silly, there's no need to kill yourself."

"At least get in the car."

"No, come back upstairs with me."

"In the car, or I'll kill myself right now." He pulled his lightweight jacket back and exposed a small handgun.

I felt like telling him to go ahead kill himself. I knew it would be stupid to get into the car with an unbalanced person with a gun.

"It's a long story, and I need someone to hear it."

What you know and what you do are sometimes in conflict. I know this every time I eat that second donut, but when things get this serious, we should all listen to our brain. I knew better than to get into that car, but my curiosity and illogical bravado overpowered my common sense. I glanced up again to see if any of the gang, my so-called bodyguards were looking down at us.

"There's no one up there," Streelman said.

He was right.

"Come on man, none of this is necessary."

"Don't make this worse than it needs to be. I could always

shoot you first. Like I said, I'm dying tonight. Your choice is how hard do you want to make it on yourself?"

I considered charging him, but we weren't close enough to each other, and he already had his hand on the weapon.

"Listen to my story or die right here. Your choice."

I could've stalled, maybe back away a little and then run. I should've kept him talking, but I didn't.

Chapter 28

Louise's phone rang as she undressed to take a shower.

"I need you at the hotel five minutes ago," Nichols said.

"What's up?"

"Everything has hit the fan. Streelman's our killer, and he has West."

"What? How? At the hotel?"

"Just get there now."

Louise looked at the phone. Nichols had already ended the call. With a dozen questions on her mind, she rushed into her duty uniform. The announcement that Streelman had killed Nelson brought a feeling of success and relief, but hearing that he had Jim, whatever that meant, felt like someone had punched her in the stomach.

How did he have West? Did they have a hostage situation at the hotel? Had he already killed Jim?

"Dammit," Louise said and wiped a tear away. "Get a grip. You're too old to feel this way." Any tears left dried up, yet, she couldn't fight the feelings. Despite knowing their relationship would exist only a few days, she had let this guy get to her. She knew he would be a memory in another day or two, but she wanted him to be a good memory, a really good one. Something she could hang onto. Something that could always make her feel good about herself. She didn't want it to be a memory of a tragedy.

She had to park in front of the Waffles and Shakes restaurant.

Half the police cars in the city sat in front of the hotel with their flashers on. She ran to the hotel and stopped when she saw the police chief in a close huddle with Detectives Nichols and Young. Nichols saw her and broke away from his boss, hustling over to her.

"Have you heard anything?" he asked.

"Me? No. What's going on?"

"I hoped he had gotten in touch with you. About twenty minutes ago, we received a call from the police in Germantown, Tennessee. Streelman sent an email to his wife apologizing for everything. She recognized it immediately as a suicide note. She tried to call, but he didn't answer so she asked the police to help."

"Have you seen the email?"

"Yes. He admitted he had killed Nelson, but beyond that it's just a bunch of beating around the bush. No explanation why."

"Where are they?" Louise asked.

"That's it. We don't know. All we do know is that Streelman called him about thirty minutes ago and asked him to meet him down here. That's the last we know. We're only assuming he met Streelman, and they went somewhere. We can't reach either of them."

"Have we located their cars?"

"Only West's. Streelman's car is gone. A receptionist inside thinks he saw two men get into a small, light green car about that time and drive off. Streelman has an older Nissan Sentra that meets the description."

"What can I do?" Louise asked.

"Wait here until the chief gets done with us, and we'll come up with some ideas. We're already doing interviews of everyone."

He walked back to rejoin Detective Young and his boss.

"Officer Strong," Tom said and approached her.

"Tom, this is crazy. What have you heard?"

"Nothing. I can't believe Jim is in any real danger. He can handle Streelman. Do you know for sure that it was Streelman who killed Doug?"

"I don't know if we can be positive about anything at the moment. Once we find Jim, things will become better understood."

"I'm surprised he hasn't called you," Tom said.

"He may yet."

"Louise!" Detective Young shouted to her. He and Nichols had moved to a nearby police sedan.

Louise excused herself and jogged over to them.

"We received word that there was a report of a shooting," Young said.

"Where?" Louise could see that Nichols was talking to someone on his phone.

"Only about a mile from here on twenty-ninth. The shooting took place in a car. Witnesses said it was a light-colored Nissan Sentra."

"Louise, you're with me," Nichols said and walked briskly away, making Louise jog to catch up with him. "I'll drive. We have a number of witnesses. They all think the passenger is still alive."

"That's good." She had a hundred more questions, but she knew they would all get answered in a few minutes.

"Fortunately, we had an off-duty officer in the ice cream parlor when the shooting occurred, and he's been able to gather and keep the witnesses there. Two families sitting outside eating their ice cream."

"You think it was West and Streelman?"

"Yes, I do, and now we know Streelman has a gun."

"A game changer," Louise said.

They pulled into the small parking lot adjacent to the ice cream parlor.

"Detective Nichols, thanks for coming so quickly."

Louise recognized Officer Bobby French, a recent graduate of the police academy. French took them over to the group of four adults and five teenagers. French informed Nichols and Louise what the witnesses had observed. A few of the witnesses nodded their heads now and then while French related what they had already told him.

"How did you know it was a gunshot you heard?" Nichols asked the group at the end of the briefing.

"We know. We hunt, and it happened close to us. Right there," one the fathers said, pointing at the intersection barely ten yards away.

"I think the round went through the car door and hit one of the cars parked along the side of the road," said a tall, lanky teenager, wearing an Atlanta Braves hat.

"They were stopped at the red light. It's under that street light, too, so we could see. As they continued through, it looked like the passenger raised his right arm a little, so he could look at it, you know," the father that spoke before said.

"At his arm?"

"Yes sir. That's what we all think." The other witnesses nodded in agreement.

They continued talking to the group until Nichols felt confident that he had all the information he could get. While Nichols thanked the two families, Louise took Officer French aside to ensure he had sufficient identifying data on everyone in the group. She told him to take a close look at the parked cars to see if the round did hit one of them. Once finished, Nichols and Louise drove off in the direction Streelman was last seen going.

"What do you think, Barry?" She rarely called him by his first name anymore.

"I don't know, but I have an awful feeling we may have two bodies to deal with tonight."

"Why take it out on Jim, though. That makes no sense."

"I don't know. It may be that Streelman thinks he could've gotten away with it and believes something West told us has focused our attention on him. Our interviews tonight were intended to make a couple of them think we had more on them than we do. Our bluff must have worked on him," Nichols said.

"So, even though we don't, didn't until now, have a primary suspect and don't have a motive, still don't, Streelman is already blaming West for our knowing he's the killer. This is seriously bad luck for Jim. It's like it's our fault."

"He had already attacked West once, so I don't think we can blame ourselves too much. Besides, we don't know if West didn't confront him and forced Streelman's hand."

"It's possible," Louise said.

Nichols suddenly pulled into a bank's empty parking lot. "Damn! He could've gone anywhere. If he's going to kill himself, it probably doesn't matter which way he goes. Call in and see if there've been any sightings of Streelman's car."

He drove the car out of the lot and started back to the hotel, while Louise verified that there had been no sightings.

"I need to get back. You and Whip take a car and head south of the city a few miles. Go through any and all large parking lots.

We have everyone looking, but I also want you two in position in case we get a lead. I'd bet my lunch Streelman headed south," he said.

"There's a lot of wet land down there. A lot of dirt roads that lead out to nowhere," she said.

"A private place to die."

Louise shook her head slowly but didn't reply. A horrible place to die, she thought.

"This hasn't gotten too personal for you?" Nichols asked.

"No. He's a good guy, Barry. I like him, but that's all." Louise didn't make eye contact, knowing Nichols might wonder why.

Louise stared out the window, telling herself to put any emotions aside. After all, she needed to remain professional. She had not known West for a week and there was only that one night. For more than one reason, she did not want Nichols to question her relationship with West.

Chapter 29

"None of these looks like his car," Whip said. He had been waiting when Louise arrived back at the hotel. They drove slowly through the strip mall's lot, the fourth one they had inspected.

"I don't think he would pull into a parking lot just off the main road to commit suicide," Louise said.

"Doesn't make sense to me either. He's out in the swamps."

The thought made Louise shiver, but she agreed with him. "If he knows the area, there are a million places." She didn't finish her thought.

"We had that guy shoot himself in the middle of a field last month. Only found him because of all the buzzards."

"Why did he take West? If he's going to end it all, why bother with anyone else?"

"You that close to him?" Whip asked.

"Not really, but I feel like he was my responsibility."

Whip studied her, and Louise guessed he knew that her comment was only half true. They had worked together long enough for Whip to read her.

"Well, I thought the guy was a jerk. Thought he could do our investigation better than we could," he said.

She also knew Whip too well to let his remarks get to her anymore. Usually, it was his blatant disregard for a victim. He had no empathy for anyone.

"No, he didn't want to be involved in this. We pushed him as did his friends. Now, it may have gotten him killed."

"Maybe he'll luck out. Maybe he wants West to hear his confession, so someone can explain to the world why he was forced to do what he did." Whip stressed the word forced to make sure Louise knew he was being sarcastic.

"Let's hope you're right."

"Yeah, the whole department will be scrutinized if West gets killed. Most of that scrutiny will be on you and Nichols, you know."

"I'm not worried about that at the moment. Let's find him first."

"Rat's chance in hell, you know," Whip said before steering them out of the lot and down toward the next one.

"I wonder if we should start looking further away from the road."

"You mean out in the farmland, or maybe the swampy areas. Not a bad idea. It's probably where Streelman is taking him, but where?"

"He must want to get to where he is going fairly quickly. I can't believe he wants to drive all night," Louise said.

"How do you think West will let this play out? He knows Streelman has a gun and has killed someone already. Will he jump him and try to get the gun?"

"Who knows. I guess it depends how urgent the situation gets."

"I'd jump him," Whip said. "Focus on the gun hand and start breaking fingers."

Louise kept her comments to herself. She hoped Whip's fantasy world never had to face reality. They drove around for another twenty minutes before a call came in from Nichols.

"We finally got a fix on West's phone. I'm sending you the coordinates. They're off the main roads, and you two are the closest. The county boys are tied up at a nasty domestic, but a state car is in the area, and will be there shortly after you."

"Got it," Louise said. Using her phone, she hit directions and selected the quickest route. "Let's go, we're only twelve minutes away."

Whip hit the gas and turned on the flashers. "Siren, too," he asked, grinning.

"No, let's not spook him."

"It's out in the boonies. Good choice," Whip said.

They turned off onto a narrow, paved road used primarily by residents. Most of the residents had small farms or lived on property that had originally been farm land. After about five miles, they took a left on what looked like an abandoned road. A layer of asphalt had cracked and worn thin over the years.

"Must be a road to what was an old plantation. Not many places to turn off." Whip slowed as they approached a dirt road leading off to the left.

"The coordinates take us straight ahead for another mile."

"Okay," Whip said and drove on.

"Turn off the flashers."

"If you're worried about his seeing us, the headlights will give us away."

"I know, but the flashers grab people's attention and the lights might not unless we hit them head on," Louise said.

"It looks like the road dead ends up ahead," Whip said.

Louise double checked the coordinates. Everything seemed right, but where was the car?

"Maybe he made him toss his phone out the window up here.

When we get there, we'll look around for it. Maybe call it again," Whip said.

"It goes directly to voice mail so it's either off or on silent mode, but it's worth a try."

"You know, it makes no sense to drive all the way out here to just have West get rid of his phone and then, what, drive back?"

"That's what I was thinking," Louise said.

"You think they're out here somewhere? Or maybe only West is?"

They stopped the car, leaving the headlights on. The pitch-black night made seeing anything difficult. With flashlights in hand, they stepped out of the car. A humid, cool breeze rustled through the leaves of the surrounding trees and bushes. Louise heard what sounded like a small animal run through some leaves on the ground. She aimed her flashlight at the sound but only saw a thick area of wild bushes.

"If he had him toss it out the window, it would be on the ground on or near the road," Whip said. He started walking slowly around the edge of the road, shining his light along the ground.

Louise started looking along the side of the road opposite Whip. She saw a number of beer cans in one spot but nothing else. She took a step deeper into the weeds to cover more ground and immediately saw something slithering away from her. She stepped back onto the pavement.

"Whip, just saw a snake over here. Be careful."

"I'm not getting off the pavement. Might if I saw a body, but not for a phone. We should call this in."

"Let me do one more check on the GPS coordinates. Maybe I can narrow it down more," Louise said.

"Be my guest, I'm getting back in the car. This reminds me of those tales we heard as teenagers about the crazy man in the swamp. He would wait for dumb people to come out alone or in couples, and then he would kill them in all sorts of terrible ways."

"I remember those, too. How about we don't tell any right now. It's spooky enough as it is."

"I see some headlights coming at us. It's way back there still, but I hope it's the state boys," Whip said, still standing by the open door of the car.

"And not your crazy guy coming out to get us?"

"You know, Louise, some of the locals are just as crazy. They may be looking at us as trespassers."

"The GPS says we are still some forty yards away from the phone." Louise looked around and again saw nothing.

Whip leaned into the vehicle and turned on the flashers. He walked over next to Louise. The flashers on the car behind came on, too.

"Not the crazies," he said.

Louise sent a text to Nichols saying they were at the location, and so far, they hadn't found anyone or the phone. She added the state troopers were arriving. The headlights of the arriving car lit up more of the underbrush in front of them. She used this extra light to search for any sign that West might have been here. As the state car angled slightly to the right and stopped, she noticed something.

"Whip, look at that," she walked away from the car and pointed.

Chapter 30

Streelman opened his car door, but before getting in he pulled the small pistol out of his beltline and held it in his left hand. Once in the car he kept the pistol in his left hand, resting on his left thigh.

"We are going to do this my way, West. You just sit and listen. Don't do anything stupid, and you won't get hurt."

"It seems to me that you are making this a lot more complicated than necessary. I'm happy to listen to your story. If you let me, I'll even take notes."

"I'm serious," he said.

"I don't mean to imply you aren't. I'm trying to tell you that I will do as you want. I don't want anyone to die tonight, especially me."

He drove the car west, away from the beach and the hotel. I had my phone in my left front pocket of my jeans, but there was no way to get to it. Luckily, I had put it on silent when Young was interviewing us and hadn't turned it out of the silent mode since.

"Doug deserved to die you know."

"No, I don't know anything. Why do you think he deserved to die? I'm guessing you killed him."

He continued driving and didn't say anything for the next minute. When we stopped at a red light at a well-lit intersection, I noticed a family sitting in front of an ice cream shop.

"If you don't want to tell me, then there's no reason for me to stay in the car," I said, and in an impulse, I reached for the door handle.

The sound of the gunshot did a lot more than deafen me. It scared me to the point that I was surprised I hadn't ruined my pants. I had looked away from him toward the door handle, so I didn't see him raise the pistol and pull the trigger. The round creased the top of my forearm, doing little damage other than gouging a shallow path through what used to be skin, causing my blood to flow freely out of my arm. I looked at the wound and clamped my left hand down on it. The wound didn't amount to much, but I wanted to stop the bleeding. I also needed to start thinking before I did anything else that might bring about a reaction from Streelman. If I had any doubts before, I now knew to take him seriously.

"Hey! If you kill me, who's going to listen to your story."

"I have nothing to lose. I don't plan to live through the night. Whether you do, depends on how you behave. That shot was a warning. You won't get another one, and you know, I can hardly miss your head from this distance."

I saw the hole in the door and wondered if the round went all the way through. We had travelled too far for me to look back and see if the round hit anyone sitting outside the ice cream shop. Sweat had formed on Streelman's forehead.

"I believe you. I also think Doug did do something bad to you. Why don't you just turn yourself in? I certainly don't plan on pressing any charges. I'm fine, and with a good lawyer, you can probably get off with manslaughter."

"Too late for that," he said. "I'd rather die."

"Come on. Death is permanent. Most everything else can be overcome."

"Not this."

"Not what?" I asked.

"I'll tell you, but not yet. When we stop."

"You've got a wife and kids. Why do you want to hurt them by killing yourself? Think about it. No one can explain your side of the story to them better than you. I'll try, but you know they'll have more questions."

"Doug was going to ruin me. He deserved to die. I begged him to let it be, but he laughed. He didn't care about my life, not one bit. So, it was really his fault. If my life meant nothing to him, how did he expect me to care whether he lived or died?"

"You're right. He was blackmailing you?"

Streelman glanced over at me. "So, you figured it out. Both Eric and Larry said you were too sharp for your own good."

"No, I hadn't figured anything out. No one had, including the police, but now they will focus on you. I was with a couple of the guys when you asked me to come down."

"That no longer matters. Don't you get it? I've already made my peace with this. I already sent an email to my wife saying good bye."

If I had any doubt about his intentions, they disappeared. "Oh, James. What do you think is going through her mind right now? How do you think she is feeling?"

"Shut up!" His left hand raised slightly and aimed the pistol at my head.

The small pistol looked to be a 9mm. Because of its short barrel, its aim was only effective at short range. Unfortunately for me, our two feet of separation was well within its effective range. His hand covered most of the pistol, so I couldn't tell the manufacturer, but I already had proof that it worked and was loaded. Nothing else really mattered.

"You ever see a guy kill himself?"

"No," I said. "Seen too many dead bodies though. I don't want to see another one tonight."

"So maybe I should kill you first? Do you a favor?"

"I don't mean that. I don't want to see you kill yourself, but staying alive is a higher priority for me. You won't be doing me any favors by killing me first. Kill me second," I said in an effort to lighten the mood.

He grinned. "Don't ask for that either. My ghost might come back and kill you. What do you think West? Is there some sort of life after death?"

"I hope so. I think so. It's always seemed illogical to me that this pile of flesh and bone we call our body created consciousness."

"All animals have some level of consciousness," he said.

"I know that, but there is a difference. At least to me there's a quantum leap from their level of consciousness to ours. Besides, why shouldn't they have some level of consciousness, as you say."

"We don't behave any better than animals."

"Worse in many cases, I agree," I said.

"So, if you think I'm going to hell, why should I care what I do from here on out?"

"I never said you're going to hell. I don't know if there is a hell or what it might be like. For one thing, James, I don't believe in easy definitions for things we don't understand."

"You don't believe in the bible?"

I didn't know where he was going with all this, but I figured keeping him talking might do some good. Maybe he still wasn't sure what he planned to do with himself or me.

"Like I said, I don't have the answers. I don't disbelieve the bible, although I have to admit I've never read the whole thing. At the same time, my understanding is that a good portion of the bible has been rewritten and retranslated enough times through the centuries to question its validity. Not the story, only the specifics."

"Yeah, people can't be trusted."

"You're preaching to the choir. I spent my career in the air force learning that. Listen, James, why don't you and I go to some hole-in-the-wall bar around here and get drunk. That would be a better way to end the night. Don't you think?"

"You should have made that offer yesterday. It's too late."

"No, it's not. You have a good reason why you attacked Doug. You can tell it anyway you want. Hell, you can spin it any way you want. No one else was there."

"I've already told you, killing Doug isn't the real issue. He's scum. You know what's interesting, West?"

"No, what?" We turned off the main road and started driving down a narrow two-lane road into an area with fields and scattered houses. He didn't answer me, so I asked, "Where are we going now?"

He ignored my question. "What's interesting is that I'm kind of looking forward to dying. It's the ultimate escape. I think it's like falling asleep and simply never waking up."

"You dream at night?"

"At times, of course."

"Think you might dream in death?"

"You can't," he said.

"You know people who have been in comas with very little brain activity dream." I figured he wouldn't know if I knew this or not. It didn't matter.

"So, they're still alive."

"Their body is still alive by a thread. Their consciousness is fine. Some later say they heard people talking around them. I think that's fascinating. It seems to support the theory how little the soul needs the body."

"What are you trying to tell me, West?"

"That death may not turn out to be the peaceful sleep you are seeking. You can't be sure, so why rush it?"

"You're wasting your breath. I brought you with me so I could tell someone my side of the story. Now you're telling me I might not want to die alone. You think if you went with me, it would be easier on me. You know, not going alone into that void." He had a very unpleasant smile that I didn't like at all.

Chapter 31

He turned off the country road to what I first thought might be someone's long driveway. The branches of large trees hung over the road, and in the darkness, I could see what looked like abandoned fields.

"We're pretty much in the middle of nowhere," I said.

"It won't be long," he said.

"Until what? James, let's stop and talk. You want me to hear your story." I didn't feel this would end well. The hairs on the back of my neck felt like they were doing the jitterbug, so I reached back to rub my neck. The movement caused Streelman to lift the pistol a couple inches off his leg.

My options were limited. He was doing fine steering with his right hand, leaving his left hand with the weapon aimed at me. I didn't think anything I could do would be faster than his pulling the trigger. I silently cursed myself for getting into the car.

"Why did you tell the police that I killed Doug?"

"What? I didn't? I didn't know who did it."

"Who was it that put you onto me? Was it LG? I always liked him, too. Never thought he would rat on me."

"You're making a lot of wrong assumptions."

"Does it matter? I'm not going to be able to talk to them again."

The road looked like it came to a dead end or maybe a tee intersection about a quarter mile ahead. A slender thread of relief drifted into me. At least the wait might be over.

"Just up here," he said.

The headlights lit up the end of the road, and I could see that we were approaching a dead end. Thick underbrush blocked the view past the road. A couple large trees shot up high straight ahead in the darkness.

Suddenly, Streelman did the unexpected. He stomped on the accelerator, and the Nissan shot forward like a quarter horse coming out of the gates.

"James!"

He ignored me, staring straight ahead. I looked and saw we were bearing down on a large oak. The car accelerated past fifty miles an hour, bouncing on the uneven road. He had dropped the pistol and now gripped the steering wheel with both hands. At the last second, I reached over and yanked the steering wheel, turning the car to the right.

The car missed the tree trunk but shot through tree branches, bushes, vines, and tall weeds. I tried to shift the car out of gear, but things happened too fast. The car went flying off the ground, and despite the increasing darkness, I saw a small river below us. We hit the slope about ten yards above the water, tearing through small trees, logs, and a variety of boulders in our final descent into the water.

At some point the air bags inflated, smashing my head back to the seat's head rest. Something broke violently through the front windshield. The entire motor assembly smashed back against my feet and shins. Something hit the roof above of the car, slamming it against my head. Streelman screamed.

I don't think I lost consciousness, but I was dazed. The feeling of cold water rising up to my knees brought me out of it. My eyes took a second to shake off the blurry filter I seemed to be looking through. The air bags had already deflated. We stopped at a forty-five-degree angle with the front end of the car under water, possibly wedged into the bottom of the river. The back of the car began settling down, resting with the front of the car still at a slight downward slant.

The front windshield had cracked in a million places, making seeing out of it almost impossible. A limb of a tree, about two inches in diameter, had punctured the glass, the driver's side air bag, and Streelman's left shoulder.

"Streelman." He didn't answer. I studied what parts of my body I could see. Other than my wounded arm, I couldn't see any other injuries. My face hurt, likely as a result of the air bag smacking into it. The dark water prevented me from seeing my legs below my knees. I couldn't move them. If the damaged motor parts that had them trapped had cut me, I worried that the dirty river water would soon be infecting them. I felt the pressure against my legs and hoped that was a good sign.

The car suddenly slipped and went deeper into the river. The water spread up to my lower chest. I removed my seat belt before reaching over and doing the same for Streelman.

"We need to get out of here."

He remained silent, but his head turned to face me. His eyes opened, startling me, but they looked like a blind man's or a dead man's eyes.

"Can you hear me? Streelman!" He didn't respond, but his eyes fluttered and closed.

I leaned over to great a better look at him. His nose had a light flow of blood oozing out of it. The only other noticeable injury was the tree limb sticking into his left shoulder. A dark stain was spreading onto his shirt all around the branch. Even in the darkness, I knew it was blood. I stretched to feel behind his shoulder. The limb had not gone through.

Grabbing the limb, I tried to pull it away from him, but it didn't budge. The limb extended out the front window for about three feet where it looked like it had snapped off its tree. Something bumped against the front of the car. With all the cracks in the windshield and the darkness outside, I couldn't see what had struck the car. I hoped it wasn't an alligator that had come to investigate.

I tried to open my door, but it wouldn't move. My side window had cracked into a thousand fragments in the crash but remained mostly intact. A diagonal piece of glass had broken away from the top right section of the window. Kicking the rest of the window out would be easy, but I first would have to free my legs. I tried in vain before deciding it would be easier to move the seat.

Streelman coughed and gagged. His right hand lifted a few inches off the center console before dropping back down into the water.

"Streelman! Hey, snap out of it. We need to get out of the car." He didn't give me any indication he heard me. "Damn you, I thought you wanted to talk. Why did you go and do this?"

I reached down to feel for the buttons to move the seat backwards. To my surprise the seat didn't have any. I hadn't been in a car without power seats for a long time. Still, one doesn't forget how manual seats work, so I pulled on the lever that allowed my seatback to recline. Other than slightly improving my comfort, the action was useless. I still couldn't move my legs.

The water that covered our legs was pitch black in the darkness and already smelled of gas or oil. I reached into it in front of my seat to find the lever that would allow me to move the seat back. The part of the car that had been forced back against my legs only allowed the narrowest slit to reach my arm through. I forced my arm down, feeling a sharp edge of metal rip my skin. When I pulled my arm back, the metal felt like it dug in deeper, so I stopped, deciding to continue to reach lower and find the lever.

"West," Streelman's voice croaked.

"Not right now."

"What happened?"

I ignored him, as my fingers finally wrapped around the lever. Unfortunately, my arm was pressed tight against the seat. My hand and fingers had to move the lever without any motion of my arm. The open space under the seat gave my hand plenty of space, and despite the awkwardness, I finally moved the lever enough to release the seat. It sprung backwards an inch or two. Not far, but enough to remove the pressure on my legs.

I lifted my arm up without tearing it anymore on the jagged edge of metal. My legs felt okay, so shook them as much as I could and wiggled my feet. Although it would still be tricky, I thought I might be able to squirm out of the car.

"I can't move," Streelman said.

"Join the club. Why did you do this?"

"I wanted to die. I think I will now, just more slowly."

"I thought you wanted to first tell me everything."

"Screw you, I lied. I wanted you to die, too."

That surprised me. Maybe it shouldn't have, because I always thought he might shoot me, but I thought he actually wanted to confess why he had killed Doug.

"We need to get out of here." I thought of my phone and dug it out of my pocket. Water dripped from it.

"Does it work?" He sounded lucid, but spoke in a strained voice.

"No, we've had water up above our waist for a while."

"Guess you don't have any rice to put it in," he started giggling. After a couple seconds, the giggling turned into coughing and gagging again.

"I'm going to try to get out, and then I'll see what I can do about you."

"I think I'm going to throw up."

"Not in here."

I tried to squirm up and off the passenger seat. I couldn't. I again tried lowering the back of the car seat as low as it would go and even repeated the effort for a third time. It didn't recline any further. If I had been made of rubber, it would've been an easy task, but my bones wouldn't bend.

"It's no use," he said.

"I'm not giving up that easy."

"I got you pretty good, didn't I?"

"Well, you're stuck here, too," I said.

"I don't mean that. Where I hit you, it's bleeding again." He actually grinned when he said that.

I touched the bandage above my eye but couldn't tell much. My hand was already wet, and the darkness made it hard to distinguish blood from the dirty, dark water.

"If this is all a joke to you, why did you have to kill yourself and take me with you. What terrible sin are you hiding?"

"It's no sin. It's something Doug should have left alone. It was my business, not his. He turned something nice into something that would ruin several lives. He intended to take all my money, too. What did he expect?"

"That last part, I agree with you. I'm sure everyone will understand, so let's get out of here," I said, trying to sound sincere.

Reaching under the seat I tried to find a lever that might allow me to remove the seat from the floor of the car, but if such a thing was there, I couldn't find it. I pushed against the section of the car that the accident had crushed against my legs, but it wouldn't move.

"Can you move your legs?" I asked.

"Nope. Don't want to, either. Hurts when I do."

I figured the best way to free my legs would be to bust out the passenger side window and to crawl out, dragging my legs and feet up and sidewise. Doing that would prevent my having to bend my legs where they didn't bend. It would still be a tight squeeze, but I thought it should work.

Not having a tool to use, I struck the damaged window with my elbow. The window cracked some more and bent out a little at the impact point. Feeling confident, I struck it again with more force. Part of the window popped out of the door, but my elbow extended out a small hole that it had made, and the safety glass still clung together around it, pinching into my arm when I tried to pull my arm free.

Cursing, I used my left hand to peel away the glass from my arm. Despite the darkness, I could see a dark fluid flowing out of the bullet wound. Spots of blood also grew in size where several pieces of glass had dug themselves through the first layer or two of skin. I used the side of my right fist to carefully pop out the rest of the window. One small, triangle shaped piece of glass remained in place at the bottom of the window. I wiggled it and tried to remove it but it wouldn't budge. Too small to hit with my fist, it remained there looking like a shark's tooth happily waiting for me to try to slide out the window.

The glove compartment wouldn't open, and my search for any type of tool failed. I maneuvered my soaking wet cell phone out of my pocket again, and after once more verifying that it was dead, rapped it against the fragment of glass. I finally managed to break most of the glass away, but a small quarter inch of jagged glass remained. It looked a lot less dangerous than it had a moment before, but I figured it would still tear my jeans and maybe rip my skin if I wasn't careful.

Streelman had passed out or died. I didn't care which; my mind focused on escaping from the car. I tried the door again, but it didn't budge. Getting out the side window turned out to be a lot more difficult than I imagined. My first obstacle was getting my head and shoulders out. The open window had enough room, but I had little leverage to use in lifting my body, especially with my legs still trapped. I had to reach out the window with both arms and use all my strength to slowly ooze my upper body through. At the same time, I tried to use my legs and feet to help, but the tight space in which they were trapped complicated things.

I managed to twist both feet and started my final push when all of a sudden, the car slid violently sideways pushing me ahead of it as the rear end of the car started to swing around in my direction. The water rose, and I felt my shoe get stuck on something as I tried to escape.

Chapter 32

Cold water splashed around me while I struggled to keep my head above it and free my foot. It only took a second or two, but by the time I pulled my foot free, I had to force my panic to subside. Standing, I discovered the water only came up an inch or two above my waist. I stood there, trying to get my bearings and spitting out the river water that had gotten into my mouth.

The darkness covered everything like a wet blanket. I could see the car and could make out the river bank, but not much else. The car had stopped moving but now tilted slightly with the passenger side lower. The current felt steady but not that strong, yet I knew what constant pressure could do.

"West," Streelman's voice barely reached me.

"I'm fine. Let me come around and get you."

"I don't want to drown. Don't let me drown."

"You should've thought about that before."

I managed to move around the back of the car to a spot outside the driver's door. I tried to open it, but like mine, it was jammed shut.

"Can you slide out my side?"

"My leg feels like it's broken, and have you forgotten, I'm kind of pinned here."

"Serves you right." I reached for the tree limb that had him pinned. I could reach it, but I couldn't get any leverage on it from my position.

"I think you have to break the windshield first. You may also have to pull from in front of the car."

I had no desire to stand in front of the car. Any second it could slide deeper into the river, pinning anything in front of it to the river's bottom. Breaking the windshield might help, so I figured to take on that first. I had stepped on a rock nearby, so I reached down, feeling around for it, but couldn't locate it. I had to duck my head into the water to reach the ground. The thought that it might have moved on its own didn't sit well with me, so I felt around more with my feet until I found it. This time I located it in my first attempt and picked it up out of the water.

The rock moved, and I saw things protruding from it. I flung it away while stepping back and almost losing my balance.

Streelman laughed. "What was that, a turtle? You're lucky it wasn't a snapper. You could've lost a finger." He laughed which brought about another attack of coughing and gagging.

"Damn you, Streelman, if we do get out of this, I will kill you." Angry, I leaned over the front of the car from the side and reached for the limb. I jerked it toward me. The window made both a crunching and a cracking sound. I pushed the limb away, then I jerked it back. This time, Streelman howled in pain. I didn't stop. I shook and jerked the limb until it came free, bringing a third of the front windshield with it.

Streelman had passed out again. A blessing, I thought, if I was going to drag him out of the car. I used the limb to break out what was left of his already shattered side window. After the car's most recent slide, the water had risen up to his armpits, but he had remained with his back flush against the seat. If he had slumped forward after I had removed the limb, he might've drowned. I had a passing urge to stick his face into the water.

Reaching in, I grabbed him under his armpits and pulled.

Right away I knew it would be more difficult than I first thought. I estimated that he weighed twenty to thirty pounds less than me and had a thin build, but my initial effort did little more than to better position him for extraction. At least the water helped. As I untangled parts of him free from the car, the river tried to float him. Still, I had to fight the awkwardness of the angles. His legs floated free easier than mine had, but I noticed his right leg bent where it shouldn't a few inches below the knee.

Streelman regained consciousness with a scream. One of his legs got caught up in the steering wheel. He twisted and fought me, yelling at me to stop.

"My leg! My leg!" he gagged and coughed again as he tried to shout. A second or two later, he passed out again.

I tried to maneuver him, but I had little to no leverage. I pulled a little slower, and his legs appeared, floating to the top of the water. Something banged against the other side of the car. I stood still, hoping once again it was a log drifting with the river's current, and not an alligator coming to check things out. After a few seconds, I took a step backwards, pulling Streelman as I did.

Suddenly, the car slid deeper into the river. Although it stopped after six or seven inches, I knew I had to get him out, and then get both of us away from the car without any further delay. The car's movement caused one of his feet to get caught between the seat back and the car. With him ninety percent out of the car, I couldn't reach his foot without letting go of his armpits. I tried to bend him into a sitting position, but that didn't help.

I decided to let go of him and use both hands to free his foot. It only took a few seconds to get it free, but he was conscious and coughing up water by the time I lifted his head out of the river.

"You tried to drown me." His voice sounded like an angry whisper.

I ignored him and looked around to locate the shore. A light fog had developed, compounding the darkness. Pulling Streelman along with me, I waded back to the car to get my bearings. I looked behind the car to where the shore should be and saw it about ten yards away.

"Next time you want to kill us, do it during daylight," I said.

"I don't think I wanted to kill you, but I didn't want to die alone, and those other guys are my friends."

"Thanks. Anything in the car you need?" I asked, knowing it was a stupid question. I wasn't going back inside.

I took a second to look inside the window. The water level now hid most of the steering wheel. Despite standing only a couple feet from the car, seeing inside was difficult. The surface of the water appeared like an opaque covering. I knew the pistol he had brought with him now lay on the vehicle's floor to be recovered later by the police.

As I turned, something caught my eye. Instinctively, I took two quick steps backward as a large snake swam through the missing window and past me. I imagined it had come in one window and straight out the other. It's head and most of its body moved silently along the top of the water.

I needed no further motivation. The last adrenalin I had left in my body surged through me, and I carried Streelman with me to the bank of the river. I didn't stop there. I'd seen too many nature shows on television with alligators leaping out of the river and dragging their unsuspecting prey back into the water. A rocky ledge blocked our progress after a few yards.

In the water, I had little difficulty in positioning Streelman over my right shoulder, but maneuvering him onto the ledge that also came up to my shoulders took every bit of my dwindling strength. Only the thought of some creature coming out of the water after me gave me the energy to climb up next to him. Once there I stretched out the best I could on the rocky surface. I didn't know how far we still had to climb, but I had to rest. A dog barked somewhere in the distance.

Civilization, I thought. What did the lyrics of that song say? "So close, yet so far away." That's how I felt.

"Ohhh," Streelman moaned.

Chapter 33

"What is it?" Whip asked.

"Over there. Their headlights are pointed at an area that looks like a car may have gone through there," Louise said.

"Oh yeah, maybe you're right, but I'm not walking in there tonight."

"Don't be a wimp, Whip."

"What do you have?" A tall, lanky state police officer asked while climbing out of his vehicle.

"Trying to trace the movements of our suspect and a man he has with him. The last fix has him here, or near here," Louise said.

"I've got that. By the way, I'm Ethan."

"Louise, and that guy over there, who's afraid of the dark, is Whip."

Ethan grinned and nodded a greeting to Whip. "You think the car went through there?"

"Could be. I can't think what else would've caused that damage to the underbrush," Louise said.

"I'm not afraid of the dark. I just think it's not advisable to walking through that in the night when we can't see anything," Whip said.

"He's got a point, besides there's a steep drop-off to the river a few yards farther in. I recommend we get a professional team out here now," Ethan said.

"That's right. That is where we are," Louise said, remembering this part of the county.

"I'm sorry, but if they went off the cliff, they're likely dead. I guess a tree may have broken their fall, but it's a ride I wouldn't take."

"I'll call it in and request a team to do the climbing and searching," Whip said.

Louise walked to the end of the pavement in the direction the car must have taken. Despite the darkness and the shadows caused by her flashlight, she discovered tire marks in the dirt a few yards off the cracked blacktop.

"Look at these Ethan."

He showed no reluctance to walk out into the weeds, and the two proceeded to where the thick bushes had been crushed down and bent sidewise. Most had tried to return to their natural position, but the damage had been done. Standing in the knee-high weeds, they both directed their flashlights further down the path the car took.

"That's where it falls off," Ethan said.

"The ground is damp. I don't suggest we get too close, or we may find ourselves slipping the rest of the way down."

"You wouldn't have to slip far to go over the edge."

"So, you don't think they could survive?" Louise asked.

"It's possible, the cliffs along here aren't straight down. If the car remained upright as it bounced along, I guess they could've survived. But then, they'd have to get out of the car before the river took them under."

"Any other way to get down there?" Louise asked.

"Not near here in the dark. Not that I know of. You could go up river a couple of miles and maybe get a boat in by the bridge. Let me call it in to my guys and ask them to do it. They may be able to reach the car faster than we can get a climb team here."

"Do it, please."

Ethan walked back to his vehicle, and Louise suddenly not liking it alone in the weeds, followed after him.

Whip approached her. "They're working it. Nichols is on his way out. Wanted to tell him it's a wasted trip. He's not going to add anything to the scene."

"I'm sure he feels useless wherever he is, so coming out here is at least something. It's getting chilly." She rubbed her hands together and thought of West. If he had survived the crash and was wet, the night may yet kill him. She felt useless, once more considering the risk of climbing down to the river.

"My guess is that we'll find the car a mile or so down the river tomorrow," Whip said, interrupting her thoughts.

"Probably," Ethan said.

"The current is not that fast, but it's steady and strong this time of year. If the car gets out to the middle, there's nothing to stop it. I don't mean to discourage you, but even if he made it out of the car alive, the river and the critters in it would end him. Hear about the kid that swam into the nest of water moccasins?" Whip asked.

"Whip, Whip, don't go there. I don't need that vision in my head. Besides that's not true. It's an old tale used to scare kids, and I don't need to hear it again," Louise said.

"It happened in that movie, Lonesome Dove."

"I know, but that was a movie, not real life."

"I think I made their night," Ethan said, interrupting them.

"Who?" Whip asked.

"The guys on shift. They liked the idea of going down the river on a boat. Otherwise, they'd be stuck in the office waiting for something to happen. A boat ride is better than responding to a truck accident on the highway."

"Guess I can't blame them for that. Can I go with them?" Whip said.

"No, we only have the one car, and you aren't taking it anywhere," Louise said.

Barely had the words come out of her mouth when she spotted the headlights of another vehicle coming toward them. When the sedan pulled up next to them, Louise saw Detective Nichols in the passenger seat and a young rookie, whom she recognized as Steve Pitts, driving him.

Nichols got out first. The rookie stayed in the car with the engine running. Louise guessed Nichols told him to keep the car running since they might only stay for a second. Nichols exchanged names and a handshake with the state officer.

"What do we have?" Nichols asked Louise.

"It looks like the car went through the undergrowth right there and over the cliff."

"Cliff?"

"Yes, Detective. It's not much of one, but there's a drop off of some thirty to forty feet. We tried to take a look, but it's too dark and the ground is damp and slippery, so we didn't get up to the edge to look over," Ethan said.

"Pitts," Nichols shouted. "Get that rope out of the trunk and come with me."

"I don't recommend trying to climb down in the dark." Ethan said.

"I don't either," Nichols said without further explanation. "Come with me." He spoke to Pitts, but everyone followed him.

"Tie one end of the rope around that tree and give me the other end."

Pitts did as instructed, and Nichols secured the other end of the rope around his waist.

"Hold onto your end and let out the slack as I walk toward the edge, but don't you let go if I slip." He smiled, "No matter how tempting."

Nichols took small steady steps. He held a flashlight in his right hand and the rope in his left. "A car definitely went through here."

"Be careful," Louise said.

"Hold on now, I'm going to lean out and try to get a look at what's below."

"Braver man than me," Ethan whispered to Louise.

"I see the car, or at least its tail lights. It's almost completely under water. No sign of life." Nichols stayed where he was for a few seconds, while he moved the flashlight's beam around on the terrain below him.

A strong tug on the rope signaled Nichols was coming back. Pitts groaned as the rope became taut. Once Nichols reached flat ground and walked toward them, he let go of the rope to untie it from around his waist. Pitts untied his end from the tree.

"There's no way to get down there from here in the dark," Nichols said.

"We figured that and have requested a boat search and rescue," Ethan said.

"Good idea," Nichols said.

"It will be leaving in a few minutes. Your officer would like to ride along if that's alright."

"You'd have to give Strong a ride back," Whip said.

"Take off. Pitts go with them. Can your boat handle two more?"

"I'll check," Ethan said.

"Do you mind driving me?" Nichols asked Louise.

"Not at all. It'll be like old days." Louise had been his driver of choice for about six months, when he first arrived years ago from North Myrtle Beach. He had served there for a dozen years but was a brand-new detective.

"The good old days," Nichols said, smiling.

Louise had enjoyed driving and working beside Nichols. At the time, Nichols' wife suffered from cancer. The two had become close, too close, and they both realized they needed to back off. Louise went back on patrol, and Nichols selected a relative rookie as his driver. Since then, he made it the norm to pick a new rookie every year to mentor and to be his driver.

Seven months ago, Nichols' wife had passed away. Louise knew she would be lying to herself if she denied wanting to rekindle their relationship. The thought surprised her when it popped into her mind. She guessed she had always known it, but had shoved it away into a corner of her mind where such thoughts did no good. First, he was married and then grieving.

Had she gotten that lonely? She told herself no, yet she had fallen for Jim a day or two after meeting him. Louise rationalized that she knew whatever happened with Jim would be short term. These things just happen. Still, had she become so easy that one smile and comment about the good old days would bring out the butterflies in her like she was still in high school?

"They can handle two," Ethan said.

"Then you two had better hurry. I assume you know where you're going," Nichols said.

Pitts didn't hesitate, jumping into the passenger seat.

"Anything you need out of the car?" Whip shouted to Louise.

She shook her head. Whip maneuvered the car around and sped down the road with the car's flashers lighting up the trees along the road.

"How's he doing?" Nichols asked.

"He'll make it."

"Ethan, do you have anyone else coming out?"

"Just the guys in the boat. I told them there was no use sending more people here tonight unless they can get a climb team here. They're working it, but I'm not too optimistic anyone will get here before the boat."

"Wish I brought some coffee. It's going to get chillier tonight," Nichols said.

"Someone else is coming," Louise said a few minutes later. "Headlights, way down the road."

"You don't think your officer turned around, do you?" Ethan said.

"I wouldn't think so, unless there was no room on the boat," Louise said.

The car moved slowly, as though the driver was in no hurry. The car's flashers suddenly lit up.

"It does look like a police car of some sort," Nichols said.

"Think they turned on the flashers so we wouldn't shoot 'em?" Ethan asked.

"Who knows, but I doubt if it's one of ours," Nichols said.

"Seems like someone's showing off," Louise said.

Chapter 34

Sheriff Dewey Barnes groaned when he stepped out the passenger door of the county's new Ford Taurus. "Pulled a back muscle wrestling with my grandkids."

An overweight deputy, who might have been older than Barnes, climbed out of the driver's side door. "Evening," he said.

Louise had met Sheriff Barnes a few times at events. His county was immediately west of Myrtle Beach. He had a reputation of being a good and fair man whose talents were in administration not the field. The stories of his walking through blood at a fresh crime scene or using the bathroom in an apartment still being processed by the forensics team were legendary.

"Evening, Sheriff. Is this your county?" Ethan asked.

"Other side of the river. I told Griff I would be coming over, and he said to have at it. Guess his boys are tied up elsewhere, and I imagine he's waiting to see if you find anything."

"Sheriff, we met in passing a while back. I'm Detective Barry Nichols and this is Louise Strong. I think we've found the car. Looks like Streelman, he's our murder suspect, drove right through here without slowing down and went over the cliff," Nichols said pointing to the tire marks.

"I do remember you. Not much of a cliff here, you know. I used to climb these cliffs as a kid. How about you, Junior?"

The deputy grinned, "All the time, but a few miles further down the river. Not safe to try it at night. It's steep enough to get you killed."

"Any of you all ever been here," the sheriff asked. After everyone said no, he continued. "This spot used to be a favorite place to come park at night. Quiet, dark, and spooky enough to heighten the desire to snuggle." He laughed at his own memories.

"That big house down the road apiece is haunted. That's what they say," Junior said.

"I've heard that," Ethan said.

"Did you say you could see the car?" the sheriff asked.

"Just barely, but it's down there," Nichols said.

"Junior, should we take a look?"

"It's slippery, and there isn't much to see," Nichols said.

"I won't go far." Sheriff Barnes took a flashlight out of his car and started following the trail of the car.

"We have a rope," Nichols said.

"Shouldn't need it," Barnes said.

"Not smart," Ethan said in a voice that Louise barely heard.

Seemingly oblivious to the risk, the sheriff plodded through the underbrush.

"Damn!" Barnes shouted. The sound of someone falling through the thick underbrush immediately followed.

"Sheriff, you okay?" Junior asked, shaking his head.

The four looked at each other. Louise thought Junior might break out laughing. Nichols took a couple steps in the direction that Barnes disappeared.

"I'm okay. I slipped." His voice cracked a little, making Louise think that maybe he wasn't okay. He also sounded further away than he should've.

"Need any help getting back?" Nichols asked.

"I don't think I can get back up. May have to continue down."

"That's dangerous, Sheriff," Nichols said.

"I have my flashlight. I slid down about eight feet of slick clay. Landed on my feet, but it's too steep to climb back up. I see the car. It's almost all submerged. Don't see any signs of life. There's another ledge I may be able to get to about five feet below me."

"It's an election year, but to be honest, he's always like this. Last month he climbed thirty feet up a tree to rescue a cat. Firemen were on the way, but he couldn't wait. They had to rescue him along with the cat," Junior said.

"Not very patient," Louise said.

"No, and he does not appreciate danger."

The sound of a tree limb cracking below them followed by the sheriff cursing interrupted them.

Chapter 35

I couldn't pick up Streelman, so I sat there on the ledge next to him. We were out of the water, but in the darkness and my hurry, I hadn't selected the best spot to put us. The rock ledge stretched about six feet on either side of me. His feet dangled off one end where the ledge narrowed. Another ledge about four feet above us protruded outward, providing cover and some protection from the elements; however, it also prevented my standing.

After studying the situation, I knew I would have to climb back down before I could find any way to continue going up. I would have to leave Streelman. Served him right, I thought, but the idea of making the climb only to end up on that long desolate road seemed like a waste of time. Besides, I was wet, cold, and so tired.

"West, West, where are you?" Streelman's voice startled me.

I wondered if I had fallen asleep or had passed out. My head throbbed, and I had started shivering in the cold. My right eye had trouble opening.

"I'm right here."

"I thought you had left me. You didn't respond. I can't see. I think I'm dying. I can't see anything."

"It's pitch black out here. I can't see much either, but at least we're out of the water now. We need to make it until the sun comes out. It'll warm up, and I can go for help."

"I don't want to die."

"Then why, oh never mind. What did you want to tell me? You might as well get it off your chest. I'm likely going to die here with you anyway," I said.

"I did it for love. That's a good reason, isn't it?"

"What do you mean love?"

"I married a beautiful, sweet woman in Brazil. We have a beautiful baby."

That floored me. "So, not simply an affair. You married someone, and you're still married here in the U.S."

"Yes. We would've worked something out sooner or later."

I doubted that. "So, Doug was blackmailing you?"

"Yes. I have no idea how he found out. I offered one payment of five thousand dollars, but he laughed at me. He said he would tell me when it was over. Five thousand would only be the start."

"Then he got what he deserved," I said, half believing it and half to keep Streelman calm.

"I wasn't running the bars or chasing prostitutes. I just fell in love. She's a good woman, very religious. So, when she got pregnant, I don't know, it was either abandon her or do the right thing."

"The right thing," I said.

I stopped talking because I wanted to yell at him, to call him an idiot. Nothing he had done in the past week, not to mention marrying a woman in Brazil when he was already married could be considered the right thing. The guy was nuts.

"Yeah."

"What's her name?"

"Flor, she's a pretty flower, too."

"You better fight to stay alive then. You've still got a few responsibilities. Even from jail you can be a father. Might be safer there for you, too. Two angry wives can be a dangerous thing."

"No. I've brought shame to them."

"Yep, that you have, but that shame will pass. You still have a lifetime to apologize, give wise fatherly advice and your love through letters. That may be very important to your kids someday."

"You really think so, West?"

"I don't know," I said. In truth, I didn't know why I even said it. I wanted to tell him to go ahead and die, get it over with, but some strange part of me wanted to keep him alive. I don't think it was compassion or anything to do with his future letter writing career from prison. Maybe the simple fact that he no longer posed a threat and hadn't yet died made all the difference I needed to hope he stayed alive. I could've left him in the car. When I carried him out, I guess I had made my decision. No forgiveness, only some sort of misplaced responsibility.

"Thanks."

"You know, some people would agree with you that there's nothing wrong with falling in love with a second woman. Tom and I were talking about it today. It may be legally wrong to marry a second woman, but falling in love is not a bad thing. I'm sure with a good lawyer you can sway a jury. Besides, Doug wanted to blackmail you. That is wrong in everyone's eyes. Hang in there, stay alive, and get a good lawyer. The rest is anyone's guess, but I think you have a good chance to get off with a minimum sentence."

He didn't respond, and a moment later, I sensed he had passed out again. I started shivering. I dreaded the thought I might have to snuggle up against Streelman to stay alive. Suddenly, a small avalanche of pebbles, dirt, and twigs landed on the ledge above my head, bouncing off to the ground below. At the same time, I thought I heard the someone swearing.

"Hello! We're down here!" My voice cracked and sounded too weak to be heard by anyone more than a few yards away.

"I'm okay." The voice sounded far away. I didn't recognize it.

"Hello. We're right below you!"

Still no answer. However, I now knew they had found the spot where the car went off the road. Someone was up there trying to get down to us. Unless they hurried, I doubted Streelman would make it.

I pulled the right leg of my jeans off my shin where it felt stuck. It came off without too much effort, but I could tell that my leg must have been bleeding. That simple inspection led me to do more. My right arm burned where the bullet grazed me. The cuts from the glass in the window felt tender. My head troubled me the most. I thought the stitches may have come loose, and feeling the top of my head, I discovered a small, swollen bump. Blood had matted my hair around it. All-in-all, the cold had me worried the most. I doubted that the temperature had dipped into the fifties yet, but I was wet, and my short sleeve shirt wouldn't offer any protection.

Wondering if the ledge would conceal us from those searching for us, I considered climbing down. However, the thought of standing so close to the edge of the river in the darkness for what could be hours didn't appeal to me. I looked out and saw what appeared to be a flashlight beam focused on the car.

The sound of something moving around on the ground close to us startled me. I instinctively drew my feet in closer to me. My eyes had become as accustomed to the dark as they could, but I didn't see anything. The light fog compounded the darkness. Whatever it was I heard stayed close to the ground, moving in the weeds and other bushes. Had we left a trail of blood behind? Was something tracking the blood trail? I forced my imagination to cool it, knowing the critter out there was likely a racoon or a possum.

I could see well enough to see a person if someone happened to walk by. I could see to the river bank and a little further. Once the flashlight beam went away, the car became invisible.

"Can you hear me?" I shouted.

Another minor avalanche a few yards to our left raced down to the river.

"Whoa! Damnation! Umph!"

Something large landed near us.

"Are you okay?"

"Ohhhh," the voice sounded weak.

Some rescue, I thought.

"Can you hear me?"

"Second, my wind," the man gasped.

I waited. Despite the dubious rescue attempt, I felt a lot better.

"I'm glad I found you. I have a boat coming. A team is up above, too. I'm Sheriff Barnes, and I'm armed so don't do anything stupid. By the way, which one are you?"

"I'm West. I don't know if Streelman is going to make it. He lost his weapon in the crash. It's in the car somewhere. I'm unarmed."

A flashlight beam lit up the ground outside the ledge. "I can't see you," Barnes said.

"Your light is hitting the ground around us. We're on a ledge. I think its hidden by another ledge right above us."

"I need to call this in."

I could hear bits and pieces of his phone conversation. Streelman remained unconscious. His breathing didn't sound right. I debated trying to wake him, but decided against it. Instead, I lowered myself off the edge onto the ground.

"Sheriff, shine your flashlight down here again."

He did. A trusting fellow, I thought, since I could've been Streelman and could've still had the gun.

"You look a mess. Are you sure you're fine?"

"Fortunately, I already have an appointment at the hospital tomorrow. What I really need right now is a hot shower."

"You and me both. Think I hurt my ankle on the climb down."

Climb down, I thought. To me it had sounded like he had fallen. He sat on the ground about fifteen feet away and five or six feet above me. A dark silhouette against a darker background.

"Sheriff," a deep voice boomed down from above.

"I'm fine. I rescued them. They're both alive but injured."

"You stay there. The boat is on its way. It should be here in fifteen minutes."

"That's Junior, my number one deputy. There's also a Detective Nichols and an Officer Strong up there. Reinforcements should be on the way, too. You know you're lucky to be alive. Were you driving?"

"No." I figured he didn't know much about what had happened, but I was happy to hear that Louise waited above us. I also wanted to laugh at his comment that he rescued us, since he needed rescuing as much as we did. However, the fact that he was sitting there talking to me and to the rest of the world was indeed comforting.

"What, he didn't see that the road ended?"

"He saw it, but he was bent on killing himself and me with him."

"It should've worked. That's a rough drop off, and there are broken limbs and car parts scattered on the path you came down. In the end, you could've drowned, the car is almost totally submerged."

"Yeah, I think the car is totaled."

He laughed. "You drug him out of the car to there?"

"Yes."

"If he had tried to kill me, I would've left him in the car."

"Believe me, I thought about it."

"Too bad the clouds are heavy tonight. We could normally get a helicopter out here."

Streelman began talking incoherently. I walked the two steps back to the ledge and peered in. He hadn't moved.

"Streelman, you awake?"

He didn't answer.

"How bad is he hurt?"

"Don't know, Sheriff. His left shoulder is busted up bad, and he is bleeding from that wound. He's also bleeding from the top of his head somewhere. His leg is broken. There could be other wounds, especially internal, but I don't know."

The flashlight lit up my face, making me squint and shy away.

"Your face doesn't look too good either."

"You're not so handsome yourself."

Barnes laughed. "Good one, but I mean your face is covered in what looks like blood." He aimed the flashlight out into the river. "Look out there."

"What am I supposed to see?"

"Those dots of light on the river surface. That's an alligator.

Not a big one, but still."

I resisted the urge to jump up on the ledge. He started talking about his youth when he played in this exact same area. Before long, we saw the light from the boat in the distance, followed shortly thereafter with the sound of its motor.

"Junior," the sheriff said into his phone. "Let them know to look for my flashlight." He paused for a while listening to Junior. "Yes, West has injuries but is mobile and alert. The other guy, Streelman, is much worse off. I'm fine, but I may have sprained my ankle." Another pause, then he continued, "Yes, and see if you can get someone from the Herald down to the bridge. Good photo op, you know." He listened for a moment longer before saying thanks and ending the call.

"Everything good?" I asked.

"Yes. That lady police officer is worried about you."

"We're friends."

"Let's see if they can see our light."

The boat had to be a quarter mile away, but Barnes aimed his flashlight at it. In a few seconds, someone on the boat aimed a more powerful beam at us.

Chapter 36

I sat alone in the hospital examination room with midnight fast approaching. Tired, they had kept me in the hospital too long, and despite the painkillers, my body hurt in too many places. I heard a soft knock on the door, and Louise walked in.

"Hi. Glad I got here before they released you."

"I'm ready to go," I said, all of a sudden feeling a little better.

"They tell me you're good to go back to the hotel tonight," she said, smiling as she sat in a chair next to me. She grabbed my hand and held it for a second.

"I have my aches and pains, but nothing major. They stitched up my arm and my head again. Washed a million scratches and gave me a shot to fend off infections. So, all-in-all, I have a dozen or so new stitches and about five pounds of new bandages on various parts of my body."

"It's a miracle you survived, but I'm glad you did. They told me you might also have a concussion."

"I don't doubt it. I can't tell you how glad I am that you were able to find us. I seriously don't know if I would've made it until morning. Wet as I was, the cold night would've been very rough."

Louise nodded. "You know, it's still touch and go with Streelman."

"That's what they told me," I said.

"They had to amputate his arm. He's banged up elsewhere, but what they're really worried about is the infection that has already set in."

I nodded, acknowledging that I heard her, but offered no response.

"We'll need a detailed statement, but that can wait until the morning. For right now, can you give me a short summary. We've figured out a lot, we think."

I walked her through how Streelman forced me at gun point to get into the car and the drive out to the river. She only asked a couple of questions for clarification until I got to the point of his telling me his secret.

"He's got a second family?" she asked, following that with a number of questions similar to the ones I had asked Streelman.

She never asked me why I bothered trying to rescue the person who had just tried to kill me. A question for which I still didn't have a good answer. When she finished, she called Nichols and gave him a shortened version of what I told her.

"Nichols is still out there. They're trying to secure the car until they can remove it from the river. It will be a long night."

"Like I said, I did not want to spend the night out there."

"At least Nichols is dry and had the good sense to take a jacket."

"I didn't exactly get an opportunity to prepare for my little adventure."

"Oh, Jim. I'm so happy you're going to be okay. I was scared tonight."

"Me, too. Did Sheriff Barnes really climb down to rescue us?"

"Ha, no way. He slipped, and then he couldn't get back up, so he decided to go down. I think he slipped and fell most of the way down. Lucky for him, he survived."

"You know he busted his ankle."

"I heard."

"Must be an election year because he was really talking up his finding and rescuing us to the press while we were getting off the boat," I said.

"He made sure the press was there, too. To be fair, he is well liked by his people. I hear they have a secret rule, though, not to ever let him be the first to a crime scene."

I smiled. I knew some of those in the air force.

"Did he say why he targeted you? You hadn't done anything to him."

"Not really, he had some misguided impression that I was a threat to his getting away with killing Doug. He also thought I had told you all to focus on him as the main suspect. Stupid man, if he would have done nothing after killing Doug, he may have gotten away with it," I said.

"Possibly. Did he really say he did all this for love?"

"Yes, but don't expect me to explain his thinking. The guy is mixed up. He told me when I first got into the car that he was going to kill himself, but first he wanted to explain everything to me, so I could tell his side of the story. Yet, he didn't. The idiot tried to kill us both without telling me anything. He only told me the rest of the story after the crash while he was in and out of consciousness."

"Your friends are all worried about you. I don't think they know much about what happened, other than that you and Streelman are both here. By morning the news stations will be all over this, but it was all too late for the ten o'clock news tonight."

"I'm not playing golf in the morning."

She laughed. "I hope not. You'll probably have trouble walking around tomorrow. Besides, I think we'll be having everyone in for one last interview tomorrow morning. We need to close as much of this out as possible before everyone leaves. I doubt if anyone will be playing golf."

A knock on the door interrupted us, and a police officer in uniform stuck his head in, motioning for Louise to come out.

"I'll be right back," she said. True to her word she returned a moment later.

"Everything okay?" I asked.

"James Streelman passed away."

I didn't respond. Too many thoughts went through my head.

"I need to step out for a while. Please don't leave the hospital before I get back."

"Okay."

She left. I looked over at my damp jeans and shirt. Putting them back on would be no fun, but I didn't think Louise brought me a change of clothes this time. My nurse showed up before Louise returned. She said I could leave and gave me a couple sheets of paper with instructions on how to keep my wounds clean. I almost turned them down, saying that I had received the same set a few days earlier, but decided it took less effort to nod my head and accept them.

I felt more exhausted than hurt. The pain medicine they had injected into me in the ambulance may have had something to do with it, but I figured that should be wearing off by now.

What a waste, I thought. For some strange reason, I felt a new anger develop inside me. Streelman caused me to miss out on what was supposed to be a fun and relaxing golf trip. I also thought about his family. I had never met any of them, but Streelman's actions would undoubtedly be devastating to them.

Maybe Nelson deserved what he got, but why here or this

week? I had a number of crazy thoughts about both Nelson and Streelman.

"Mr. West, Mr. West."

I must have fallen asleep. The nurse had a tight grip on my arm.

"Are you alright?" she asked.

"Yes, just tired I guess."

"I thought you'd be gone by now, so I came back in to check on you. Glad I did. We better check your vitals one more time before you go."

"I'm fine," I said, but she looked at me like she had heard that too many times before.

As she was taking my blood pressure, Louise came back in.

"Is everything okay?"

"Yes, a few final checks, that's all," the nurse said. "You're not driving yourself to your hotel, are you?"

"No, I'll take him back," Louise said.

Chapter 37

I sighed in relief when I saw Myrtle Beach in my rearview mirror. The morning news on the local television channel gave the story first billing and a full five minutes of coverage. Sheriff Barnes received more credit than he deserved. Nichols received little more than an acknowledgement that he was the lead investigator. I don't think he cared, he looked uncomfortable in front of the camera in his ten second interview. They mentioned Streelman by name. Thankfully, the story only referred to me as a kidnap victim, not identifying me by name.

Earlier, during breakfast, I saw a number of the guys. Most seemed genuinely concerned for me. They all wanted to know what happened. I didn't feel much like talking about it, but in the end, it was easier to do so than to try to fend off all the questions. So, while trying to eat breakfast, I had to relay the whole story to the group. Tom had already heard it in the room and readily filled in if I skipped over something too fast. I heard a few "poor James" but not too many. A few, up to last night's incident, still didn't believe that one of their own had killed Doug.

A couple of the guys surprised me by saying, "I thought it was him." I felt like saying that they should have told the police, but I imagined there was a big possibility they were trying to impress the others and likely had no idea.

I didn't see Viv. I wondered if she might find closure now, but does one more person dead really do that?

Streelman's death freed us all to leave. I had to make a final statement at the police station, but we all knew there was little left to investigate. Despite having one day left, only two of the original sixteen planned to stay and play golf. I doubted if the group would return any time soon.

After being released from the hospital the night before, Louise had given me a ride back to the hotel. We both hinted around about going to her place to spend the night. I think we both wanted to, but she knew it would've been very unprofessional. She was answering a call about every five minutes on something about the investigation. Timing was terrible. For my part, I had the desire, but I also wanted desperately to take a hot shower and go to sleep.

I learned from Nichols that my pulling the branch out of Streelman's shoulder is what likely resulted in his death. The branch had pulverized his collar bone and shattered his shoulder, but worse yet, it collapsed a large vein from his arm to his heart. When I removed the branch, the internal bleeding increased, and dirty river water washed into the large open wound. The proximity of the wound to his heart also had something to do with the severity of the infection.

If I hadn't removed the branch, I couldn't have pulled him out of the car. If I left him in the car, he would've drowned. Besides, he put us in that situation. No way I would feel guilty over his death, but still, somewhere in the back of my mind, it did bother me. The whole thing was senseless, stupid. He ruined a lot of people's lives, and now, his suffering was over. All this for love.

A strange thought crossed my mind. For some reason, I wondered if both of his families would show up at his funeral. I don't know why I was bothered by this. It had nothing to do with me, and I imagined the thought was some kind of collateral emotional damage that would bother me for a while. A shrink would have a field day with me, but for now I knew I would suffer alone.

Chapter 38

Despite wanting to put it all behind me, while driving I found a local AM station on the radio to catch any updates. Rather than reporting on the investigation, the topic for the moment focused on sports. The announcer rattled off the regional qualifiers for the upcoming state amateur golf tournament. I was happy to hear that both Jack and Cory, the two young men who had interrupted the attack on me in the parking garage, had both qualified for the big match.

That was great news. Insignificant when it came to murder and death, but still, it managed to change my mood for the rest of the day's drive. Now, if I could only learn to keep my head down on those short chip shots, maybe I could be a contender.

Title: *Dead Men Can Kill*™
- Author: Bob Doerr
- Publisher: TotalRecall Publications, Inc.
- Paper Back: ISBN: 978-1-59095-759-2
- Book: ISBN: 978-1-59095-761-5
- Number of pages: 320
- Publication: December 8, 2009

When Jim West, a former Air Force Special Agent with the Office of Special Investigations, moves back to New Mexico, his goal is simple: start an easy going second career as a professional lecturer on investigative techniques to colleges and civic organizations. He never envisioned that his practical demonstration of forensic hypnosis on stage with a state university student would stir up memories of an 18-year old murder mystery. When the student is murdered three days later, West finds himself ensnared in a web of intrigue that pits him and the small town's authorities against a ruthless, psychotic killer.

An aggressive reporter for the town newspaper seeks out West for help with the story, but after one of her co-workers is murdered, she quickly aligns her efforts with West and the Sheriff. As West works closely with her, he begins to wonder if this could be the first real relationship for him since his devastating divorce a few years earlier.

The killer, though, has other plans for the reporter and the story takes fascinating twists and turns, leading to an inevitable, riveting confrontation.

Look out for a new hero on the mystery/thriller landscape! Jim West, retired military investigator, is resourceful, intuitive, pragmatic and always competent. All of West's abilities are tested when he matches wits with psychopathic serial killer William White, a man whose appreciation for murder is surpassed only by his delight in domination. Bob Doerr has crafted a must-read addition to the genre in Dead Men Can Kill, which evolves from absorbing story to absolute page-turner as West closes in on a killer who is supposedly dead. Highly recommended!

--Dallin Malmgren, author of...
The Whole Nine Yards The Ninth Issue Is This for a Grade?

A Jim West™ Mystery/Thriller

Title: *Cold Winter's Kill*™

- Author: Bob Doerr
- Publisher: TotalRecall Publications, Inc.
- Paper Back: ISBN: 978-1-59095-763-9
- Book: ISBN: 978-1-59095-764-6
- Number of pages: 288
- Publication: Dec 8, 2009

Cold Winter's Kill is a fast-paced thriller that takes place in the scenic mountains of Lincoln County, New Mexico and throws Jim West into a race against time to stop a psychopath who abducts and kills a young blonde every Christmas...

It was one of those phone calls former Air Force Special Agent Jim West never wanted to receive--an old friend calling to ask if he could drive down to Ruidoso, New Mexico to help locate his daughter who has disappeared while on a ski trip with friends. Jim found himself heading to Ruidoso even though he believed, much like the local authorities, that if she had gone missing in the mountains in December, her survival chances were slim. He didn't want to be there when they found her, but still he drove on.

Once in Ruidoso, Jim discovers a sinister coincidence that changes everything. It appears that someone is abducting and killing one young blond every year around Christmas. The race is on--can Jim locate his friend's daughter in time? But why is this happening and who's doing it?

Jim can't wait for the local authorities to raise the priority of their search, or for the pending blizzard to pass. In his haste he puts himself in the killer's sights. Will he, too, suffer from a cold winter's kill?

"**GREAT SUSPENSE!** In *Cold Winter's Kill* Bob Doerr grabs your attention from the beginning and holds it until the last sentence. Hard to put down!"

> *--Shelba Nicholson*
> former Women's Editor, *Texarkana Gazette*

A Jim West™ Mystery/Thriller

Title: *Loose Ends Kill*™

- Author: Bob Doerr
- Publisher: TotalRecall Publications, Inc.
- Paper Back: ISBN: 978-1-59095-718-9
- Book: ISBN: 978-1-59095-719-6
- Number of pages: 288
- Publication: Oct 27, 2010

LOOSE ENDS KILL **is a fast-paced mystery/thriller** that takes place in the historic city of San Antonio, Texas, and throws Jim West into the middle of a police investigation of the murder of an old friend's wife. The police already believe they have the killer in custody – West's friend.

West is drawn into this mystery by a call from the old friend who requests his assistance. West agrees to help his friend and digs deep to try to find another suspect. In the process he soon discovers that he is being followed and targeted for harassment, but by whom?

West quickly discovers that he didn't know his old friend's wife as well as he thought. To his surprise, he learns that she has had a number of affairs dating back for more than a decade. In fact, while investigating the murder, he realizes that his friend and he may be the only two people unaware of her philandering behavior.

Theorizing that one of her lovers could have had just as much motive as her husband, West starts turning over the rocks identifying one lover after another. In doing so, West unintentionally ignites an outbreak of more death and mayhem. The police and his friend's lawyers want West to go back home. The police even threaten to arrest him.

Soon, West believes the real killer wants him gone or dead. Deciding the only way to resolve the case before the outside pressures force him to leave, he sets a trap for the killer using himself as bait. However, he soon learns he may have only outsmarted himself.

A Jim West™ Mystery/Thriller

Title: *Another Colorado Kill™*
- Author: Bob Doerr
- Publisher: TotalRecall Publications, Inc.
- Paper Back: ISBN: 978-1-59095-785-1
- Book: ISBN: 978-1-59095-786-8
- Number of pages: 288
- Publication Date: September 06, 2011

It was supposed to be a short, fun golf outing, but when Jim West and his friend Edward "Perry" Mason stumble across a dead body in a restroom at a rest stop along I-25, things turn bad and then only get worse.

With the golf outing shot, West intends to stay in Colorado Springs only for a day or two. However, when two more murder victims turn up – one with West's name handwritten in her notebook - the heat on West skyrockets. The police instruct him to stick around, and soon he discovers that while the police may want to pin the crimes on him, the killer wants him out of the picture. Way out – like dead.

West's only ally is Lieutenant Michelle Prado, a tall red head with large green eyes that captivate West. Assigned to keep an eye on West, Lieutenant Prado decides the best way to do so is to keep him close. West and Prado do their own digging into the investigation. In the process, Jim wonders how close their relationship will evolve.

It seems to West that as the police focus less on him, the killer intensifies his focus on him. Barely surviving an initial confrontation, West realizes he must take the initiative. If he doesn't, or perhaps even if he does - he may end up as just another Colorado kill.

A Jim West™ Mystery/Thriller

Title: *No One Else To Kill*™
- Author: Bob Doerr
- Publisher: TotalRecall Publications, Inc.
- Paper Back: ISBN: 978-1-59095-423-2
- eBook: ISBN: 978-1-59095-424-9
- Number of pages in the finished book: 352
- Publication Date: December 4, 2012

No One Else to Kill, **Bob Publications** - In this newest West series, Mr. West finds Doerr, TotalRecall book in the popular Jim himself stood up and out of town. Looking forward to some R & R he keeps his reservation at the remote hunting lodge. Located in the Pecos Wilderness area in New Mexico it's a hunter's haven. Expecting to do nothing other than relax, he has no idea what the rest of the weekend holds for him. When a murder takes place, the hotel guest are detained and no one is beyond suspicion. The sheriff is called in, and while the investigation is underway, a second murder takes place. Both crimes are clearly related, but by whom and why? With time running out and unable to find a motive, the legal experts seek Jim's help.

The cover for *No One Else To Kill* **is a 2013 finalist for the da Vinci Eye award.**

Bob's four previous novels in the series are titled *Dead Men Can Kill, Cold Winter's Kill, Loose Ends Kill,* and *Another Colorado Kill.* The latter two were selected as Eric Hoffer Award finalists for 2010 and 2011, respectively.

Bob Doerr's *No One Else To Kill* was awarded the Grand Prize in the "Books With Out Publishers" writing contest at www.ultimateherocontest.com

A Jim West™ Mystery/Thriller

Title: *Caffeine Can Kill*™
- Author: Bob Doerr
- Publisher: TotalRecall Publications, Inc.
- Paper Back: ISBN: 978-1-59095-562-8
- eBook: ISBN: 978-1-59095-563-5
- Number of pages in the finished book: 240
- Publication Date: 2017

This Jim West mystery/thriller, the sixth in the series, finds Jim traveling to the Texas Hill Country to attend the grand opening of a friend's winery and vineyard. Upon arriving in Fredericksburg, Jim witnesses a brutal kidnapping at a local coffee shop. The next morning while driving down an unpaved country road to the grand opening, he comes across an active crime scene barely a quarter mile from his friend's winery. A Fredericksburg policeman who talked to Jim the day before at the kidnapping scene recognizes Jim and asks him to identify the body of a dead young woman as the woman who was kidnapped. Jim does, and as a result of this unwelcome relationship with the police is asked the next morning to identify the body of another murdered person as the man who had kidnapped the young woman. A third murder throws Jim's vacation into complete disarray and draws Jim and a female friend into the sights of one of the killers.

A Jim West™ Mystery/Thriller

Title: *Greed Can Kill*™
- Author: Bob Doerr
- Publisher: TotalRecall Publications, Inc.
- Paper Back: ISBN: 978-1-59095-731-8
- eBook: ISBN: 978-1-59095-741-7
- Number of pages in the finished book: 280
- Publication Date: 2017

This adventure finds Jim traveling to Fabens, TX, in an effort to locate an old acquaintance who had written Jim a cryptic letter asking for his help in finding a briefcase. In Fabens, he discovers that someone has murdered his friend. Jim provides a copy of the letter to the local police explaining that he has no idea where the briefcase is or how to decipher the sets of numbers provided in the letter. Figuring there is nothing more he can do, Jim starts his trek back home. He plans to spend a night or two relaxing at the Lodge in Cloudcroft, NM, on his way only to find that he is being followed. An ominous, unidentified phone caller gives Jim an ultimatum - find the briefcase and turn it over to him within a week.

A violent confrontation in Cloudcroft verifies Jim's worst suspicion, a Mexican drug cartel wants the briefcase. The confrontation also brings the FBI into the picture. They also want Jim to continue his search. The search takes Jim to the New Mexican ghost town of Chloride where the final confrontation takes place and Jim finds out who the bad guys really are.

A Jim West™ Mystery/Thriller

Title: *Honeymoons Can Kill*

- Author: Bob Doerr
- Publisher: TotalRecall Publications, Inc.
- Paper Back: ISBN:
- eBook: ISBN:
- Number of pages in the finished book:
- Publication Date: 2022

Honeymoons Can Kill is a 68,000 word mystery thriller that is set on a cruise ship in the Gulf of Mexico. The eighth book in the Jim West series, this is the first book to bring back prior characters from previous books. Deputy Rose Luna (Greed Can Kill) joins Jim on a five day cruise out of Galveston, TX, and on the second day of the cruise, the couple encounters Sarah Stone (Dead Men Can Kill). Sarah Stone is now Sarah Lassiter having gotten married on the ship right before it left port. When Sarah's new husband is murdered on the second night of the cruise, the cruise changes from a relaxing vacation to a race to catch the killer before everyone disembarks in three more days. The book should be considered as rated PG-13.

Title: *Double Bogeys Can Kill*™

- Author: Bob Doerr
- Publisher: TotalRecall Publications, Inc.
- Paper Back: ISBN:
- eBook: ISBN:
- Number of pages in the finished book:
- Publication Date: 2022

This adventure finds Jim traveling to

A Jim West™ Mystery/Thriller

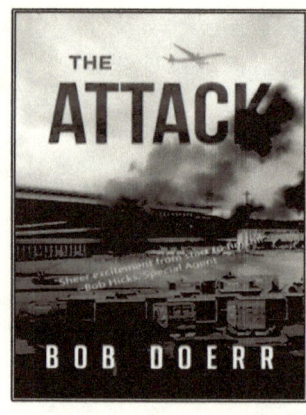

Title: *The Attack*™

- Author: Bob Doerr
- Publisher: TotalRecall Publications, Inc.
- Paper Back: ISBN: 978-1-59095-146-0
- Book: ISBN: 978-1-59095-147-7
- Number of pages in the finished book:
- Publication Date:

A terrorist team has just set off four explosive devices in an international airport close to New York City. The leader of the terrorists, Ahmad Khalin, survives the attack and plans to attack a second U.S. airport within the month. As Khalin makes his escape from the New York area he is involved in a shooting in Connecticut. Clint Smith, a U.S. government agent assigned to an ultra-secret agency, is at a restaurant across the street when the shooting occurs. He responds to the scene to see if he can help, but Khalin is gone. On a hunch, Teresa Deer, Smith's boss, sends Smith after Khalin. Smith's pursuit takes him to Bar Harbor, Maine; Wiesbaden, Germany; the Costa Brava, Spain; Northern Scotland; Lake of the Woods, Ontario, Canada; and finally into Saskatchewan, Canada, where the final confrontation takes place. Throughout the pursuit, a number of interesting characters add to the subplots and try to survive their involvement in the chase.

A Clint Smith Thriller™

Title: *The Group*™
- Author: Bob Doerr
- Publisher: TotalRecall Publications, Inc.
- Paper Back: ISBN: 978-1-59095-569-7
- eBook: ISBN: 978-1-59095-570-3
- Number of pages in the finished book: 288
- Publication Date: 2016

A fast-moving international thriller that pits a lone government operative, known as a hunter, against an unknown group of assassins who pose a worldwide threat.

Someone is killing off the world's rich and famous. The murders are sophisticated, requiring precision and skill. The international community is in an uproar but has no leads in its attempt to find the assassins. The victims were members of the Bilderberg Group, an international, loose knit group of the uber rich that meet annually. While the attacks have not had a direct impact on the U.S., Theresa Deer, Director of the Special Section, a small unit whose existence is known by only a handful in the U.S. government, sees this new age League of Assassins as a national threat. She sends her hunters out. Clint Smith finds their trail Switzerland where his discovery almost leads to his own death. The hunt leads him to Mallorca, Spain, where he witnesses a helicopter attack on a villa where a number of attendees from the Bilderberg conference were holding a follow-on meeting of their own. Smith picks up the trail a couple weeks later in Las Vegas, NV, and in his hunt finds out that he is no longer the hunter. He has become the prey.

A Clint Smith Thriller™

Title: *The Assassins*™
- Author: Bob Doerr
- Publisher: TotalRecall Publications, Inc.
- Paper Back: ISBN: 9781590951965
- eBook: ISBN: 9781590951972
- Number of pages in the finished book: 242
- Publication Date: 2018

A disputed election has divided the nation, and a handful of senior government officials have conspired to have the North Koreans assassinate the President of the United States. Believing the assassination attempt to be only days away, Theresa Deer, Director of the Special Section, a small unit whose existence is known by only a few in the U.S. government, is tasked to interdict the man intent on providing the North Koreans vital information about the president's itinerary for his visit to South Korea. While Deer succeeds in her mission, she is severely injured and finds herself being hunted by the North Korean assassins. Clint Smith is sent to Korea to help Deer get back to the U.S. and finds himself caught in a deadly game of cat and mouse with the North Koreans. With no one in the U.S. government to turn to for help, and the South Koreans now also hunting them, getting out of South Korea alive is looking unlikely.

A Clint Smith Thriller™

Title: *The Treasure* ™

- Author: Bob Doerr
- Publisher: TotalRecall Publications, Inc.
- Paper Back: ISBN: 9781648830846
- eBook: ISBN: 9781648830853
- Number of pages in the finished book: 242
- Publication Date: 2021

The Treasure is the fourth book in the Clint Smith thriller series. After a successful mission in South America, Clint heads to Las Vegas on vacation and to dig up a stagecoach strong box he had found in the desert earlier but had not opened. Upon inspection, he finds some old gold coins in mint condition and some well-preserved documents. He gives the contents of the strong box to a lawyer to find buyers. One of the documents, unfortunately, creates a maelstrom of violence and murder, and puts Clint squarely in the cross hairs of some Chinese assassins. Clint leaves Las Vegas to keep out of the spotlight, only to find himself going to Alaska in an attempt to rescue a female police officer who had been assigned to protect him in Las Vegas.

A Clint Smith Thriller™

Title: *The Enchanted Coin*™

- Author: Bob Doerr
- Publisher: TotalRecall Publications, Inc.
- Paper Back: ISBN: 978-1-59095-084-5
- Book: ISBN: 978-1-59095-085-2
- Audio Book Available:
- Number of pages in the finished book: 130
- Publication Date: September 17, 2013

We have all heard of tales of UFO's, ghosts, people who say they can talk to the spirits, ancient curses, and magical talismans. Most of us automatically dismiss them as false, figments of people's imagination, and understandably so. However, might not just a few of them be true? I don't know, but I heard this story from a young man the other day who swore the fascinating tale I have set forth in this book really did really occur, because it happened to him. You be the judge.

Title: *The Rescue of Vincent*™

- Author: Bob Doerr
- Publisher: TotalRecall Publications, Inc.
- Paperback, 6" x 9" ISBN: 978-1-59095-279-5
- eBook: ISBN: 978-1-59095-280-1
- Audio Book Available:
- Number of pages in the finished book: 160
- Publication Date: October 28, 2014

The Rescue of Vincent: Book 2 in The Enchanted Coin Series is a 31,000 word fantasy adventure targeted at Middle Grade readers. Imagine being a fourteen year old again and finding a coin that seems to give off a light of its own. The coin has your name on it, and instructs you to toss it into a fountain next to the Tree of Life. That's what happens in *The Rescue of Vincent*, and what starts my protagonist off on a magical adventure that many young boys and girls would love to have. This book is "G" rated.

Title: *The Magic of Vex*™

- Author: Bob Doerr
- Publisher: TotalRecall Publications, Inc.
- Paper Back: ISBN: 978-1-59095-309-9
- eBook: ISBN: 978-1-59095-280-1
- Audio ISBN: 978-1-59095-281-8
- Number of pages in the finished book: 140
- Publication Date: August 4, 2015

Samantha Gillespie's discovery of a magic coin results in her transportation to the strange world of Vex where magic is real and where she has to over-come a number of challenges if she ever hopes to return home.

What happened to Samantha was totally unexpected and quite frightening. It led her to an adventure that many might think impossible to believe, but it did. You be the judge.

This book is "G" rated.

Title: Stranded in Space ™

- Author: Bob Doerr
- Publisher: TotalRecall Publications, Inc.
- Paper Back: ISBN:
- eBook: ISBN:
- Number of pages in the finished book:
- Publication Date:

Stranded in Space: Book 4 in The Enchanted Coin Series is a 31,000 word fantasy adventure targeted at Middle Grade readers. Imagine being a fourteen year old again and finding a coin that seems to give off a light of its own. The coin has your name on it, claims to be magical, and instructs you to toss it into a fountain next to the Tree of Life. That's what happens in Stranded in Space, and what starts my protagonist off on a magical adventure that many young boys and girls would love to have. You be the judge.

This book is "G" rated.

Titles by Bob Doerr

Mystery Detective Suspense Thrillers

Dead Men Can Kill

Cold Winters Kill

Another Colorado Kill

Loose Ends Kill

No One Else To Kill

Caffeine Can Kill

Greed Can Kill

Honeymoons Can Kill

Double Bogeys Can Kill

Action Adventure Series

The Attack

The Group

The Assassins

The Treasure

Mouse Gate Series

The Enchanted Coin

The Rescue of Vincent

The Magic of Vex

Stranded in Space

Author Bob Doerr Uses his special knowledge
to provide authentic details in his novels
about how law enforcement agencies do their work.

For a complete list of books by Bob Doerr,
a preview of upcoming titles and more
visit his website.
www.bobdoerr.com

www.ingramcontent.com/pod-product-compliance
Lightning Source LLC
Chambersburg PA
CBHW020721130726
47899CB00011B/643